19. AUG. 1988

JET BRIGHT

JET BRIGHT
DOLLY SCANNELL

PIATKUS

Copyright © 1985 by Dolly Scannell

First published in Great Britain in 1985
by Judy Piatkus (Publishers) Limited of London

Typeset by Phoenix Photosetting, Chatham
Printed and bound in Great Britain by
Mackays of Chatham, Ltd

British Library Cataloguing in Publication Data

Scannell, Dorothy
  Jet bright.
  I. Title
  823'.914[F]   PR6069.C3/

ISBN 0-86188-314-4

'Thomas Bright's infant sister is being christened on Sunday next,' announced the Reverend Absalom Fox to his younger sister one evening at dinner.

Amelia was startled.

'Thomas Bright's sister? Are you sure?'

'Of course I am sure, Amelia. Mrs Bright arranged it when she was churched some time ago.'

'But I understood her to be a widow, Absalom.'

Absalom shrugged. 'Well she has an infant to be christened and I should imagine it's hers, for I've entered her name as the mother in the church register.'

Amelia was silent, digesting this news. She was certain Thomas's mother was a widow. She recalled the evening when Hugh Neale, the forester, had come to the Rectory to supper. He had been lodging with the Brights and had become interested in the eldest child, Thomas, a boy of high intellect. He was anxious the child should be helped and had enlisted the aid of the Revd Fox and his sister. Hugh Neale had spoken of the tragic death at sea of Mr Bright and the plight of the widow with a young family. Amelia had wondered at the difference between Thomas and his brothers and sisters, physically and intellectually. Could there be

1

some other man lurking in the background who appeared from time to time?

Normally disinterested in her brother's parishioners, because of Thomas, the Bright family had intrigued her. Judy, the beauty, was easily explained. Amelia had met Mrs Bright senior, and Meg and the twins, William and Walter, were like their uncles Daniel and Albert Hilton. She wondered who the new baby was like. Her mind went to the forester, Hugh Neale. She'd been quite taken with Mr Neale. She knew he'd lodged with Polly Bright for a long time. Surely . . . ? She stopped thinking, and said to her brother, 'I think you should ascertain who is the father of the child.'

Absalom was miles away, dreaming as usual. 'Father? What child?'

'The Bright child, of course, the one who is to be christened on Sunday.'

'Oh, I did ascertain the names of the godparents naturally, but one doesn't ask, "Who is the father of this child?"' Absalom thought for a moment and then said, 'One assumes the father is the woman's husband.'

'Well, and what if the woman has no husband yet brings her child to be christened? Do you not give spiritual guidance? Is it not your job?'

Absalom fidgeted uncomfortably. 'You worry me at times, Amelia. Do you think I am not a good parish priest?'

Amelia was sorry she'd worried her brother. After all, she was just being curious about something which was really none of her business. She wondered if more than a tinge of suspicion had led her to suspect the role of Hugh Neale as more than a lodger in the Bright household. Perhaps she was a trifle envious, if her suspicions were correct, of the innocent charm of Polly Bright. That men were weak where women were con-

2

cerned, she had always been led to believe, although her cold father, the Dean, must have been the exception to the rule. She smiled at the thought.

She got up and patted her brother on the head. 'I think you are an excellent parish priest, dear brother. Forgive me for my petty enquiries. Really the whole matter is no concern of mine and I am ashamed of my display of feminine curiosity.' Absalom smiled with relief at his sister's withdrawal of what he had believed was criticism of his capabilities.

'Feminine curiosity!' He laughed. '*You* Amelia!'

He sounded so incredulous that Amelia said briskly, 'I think I'll take Punch for a walk.' Punch was their old King Charles spaniel. He just adored Absalom, especially when he had a parishioner in his study; he liked to be part of the seminar. He'd dash in and make a great fuss of the visitor. When people remarked what an exceptionally friendly animal was Punch (he almost spoke when he gazed at Absalom) the vicar would say, 'He is indeed. Punch would do anything for me if only I could make him understand what it is I want him to do.' The visitors always laughed at the Reverend's remark and made Absalom feel he was a real humorist.

Absalom watched his sister walk down the drive with a reluctant Punch. He had hoped that now she had an interest in helping young Thomas Bright she might have settled comfortably with him and engaged herself in the life of the parish. He adored his sister, a stronger character than her brother. She had protected him in so many ways from their father. She, the intellectual child, had educated herself while helping her brother and now she wanted to go to university for herself.

They were both comfortably off, Absalom inheriting his parents' estate. Amelia inheriting a maiden aunt's estate. Absalom was content in his little backwater, looking after his parishioners was something he was capable of doing well. He wished for his sister's happiness too, even though it would leave a large gap in his life when she left.

Amelia had insisted Punch should come with her; she didn't want to walk on her own. She was feeling dissatisfied, gloomy. Absalom didn't really need her and he could manage Thomas Bright on his own without her help. She was getting in a rut and becoming indolent and petty in this lazy, cosy place. It was settled. She'd make her plans in the next few days.

Before she left, Amelia knew that she must do something about the trunks of clothes belonging to her late mother and aunt. She had been lazy about sorting them out. There would be no problem as to disposal, they would be received with great joy by many of her brother's parishioners.

Enlisting the aid of Mrs Gooch, the cook/house-keeper, Amelia soon got things organised. Mrs Gooch knew which families in the village would be overjoyed with the discarded garments. Amelia began to feel like a lady bountiful. It was when they discovered the christening robe that Amelia's thoughts turned again to Polly Bright's new babe.

The ivory-coloured gown of parchment silk and Honiton lace, beribboned and frilled, was a work of art. Mrs Gooch was horrified that Amelia wondered, innocently, if any village babies were ready for baptism.

'Them sorts of gowns is always kept in a family, Miss, from one generation to another.'

'Oh well, neither my brother nor I will ever need such a garment, and neither of us is sentimental in any case.'

'Well then, Miss Fox, there's Mrs Bright up at the

4

Dower House. Her baby's due for christening. I know her Judy had a beautiful gown but Mrs Bright, her mother-in-law, who had it made for Judy, took it back to keep for Judy's children one day. If I know Polly Bright she'd never ask for the loan of it even though it would be for Judy's sister. She'll make one out of something, Polly will.'

'That's settled then. This new baby Bright shall have a christening gown fit for a princess. I'll pack it up and get Porlock to drop it in at the Dower House.'

When Polly received the lovely gown she broke down and cried. So much had happened to her in the past four years. The death of her mistress. The fear of the workhouse with her five children. Relief that she would be able to stay at the Dower House as caretaker, a permanent roof over their heads at last. Then the advent of Hugh Neale with whom she'd fallen in love and whose baby daughter Bridget was to be christened without the presence of her father, or even the knowledge of outsiders that Hugh was the father of Polly's love child.

Hugh was married to a wife who was in a mental home. He would never abandon or neglect this wife. He was a man of strong principles. He'd never wanted to leave Polly with a child . . . but it had happened. He was deeply and irrevocably in love with her and did what he could to support his child. He was sad that his work took him to the other side of the country and he wouldn't see his daughter grow up from day to day. Financially he would have a hard time. He also knew that there was a chance he would have to go to Canada for some years just to obtain more money, and he lived for Polly's letters. He knew, too, that his baby Bridget would have to be known by the surname of Polly's dead husband, Philip Bright. One day perhaps he could

5

explain the circumstances to his daughter. Perhaps, too, ask her forgiveness.

Polly showed the robe to Mrs Plumb, her good friend and neighbour.

'Oh Poll, it's beautiful. Made for a rich lady's baby. Wonder what made the rector's sister want to part with it? Perhaps she means you only to borrow it. It's a mystery. Still some of these high-bred people do strange things. What will you do Poll? You can't refuse it, can you? In any case our Bridget'll look as good as any rich baby in it, won't she?"

Polly wanted this beautiful christening robe for her baby more than anything she felt she'd ever wanted before. She would get the money somehow and send Hugh a photo of his daughter in the wonderful robe. She was a beautiful baby, with Polly's golden colouring but Hugh's features. Suddenly she wanted for her daughter a godmother who was different from the godmothers of her other children. She wondered if Miss Amelia Fox would be a godmother – and would it mean confiding in the young lady about Hugh? No, she couldn't do that.

However, the christening robe had caused strange feelings within Polly's breast and she wrote straight away to Miss Fox to thank her for the wonderful gown. She said she would accept it as a loan and be very careful with it, and she wondered if Miss Amelia would like to see the baby.

Amelia showed the letter to her brother.

'Oh that was a kind gesture on your part, Amelia. The gown obviously means a great deal to the baby's mother. Shall you go and see the infant?'

To Absalom's surprise, and indeed to her own, Amelia said she would go that very day.

'It would be good', said Absalom, 'if the child had a

6

godmother to watch over it conscientiously. So many godparents are just names for the christening ceremony alone.'

'What a strange thing for Absalom to say to me of all people,' thought Amelia. Looking back afterwards she wondered if finding the christening gown was the key which unlocked the door to a very different life from the one she had ideally envisaged for herself.

The following Sunday Amelia found herself at the font in her brother's church, making promises for the beautiful babe in her arms. Amelia, godmother to Bridget and future friend of the family, accepting Polly and being accepted.

Thinking over the events that evening, she was puzzled that it had happened, but somehow pleased that she had a sense of belonging now. She would look forward to her return to Great Little Tisbury during her holidays from college.

But, not for the first time, her departure was delayed by unforeseen happenings.

Amelia was reading when she heard sounds of a scuffle – shouting, screaming and banging from the direction of her brother's study. She hurried from the drawing-room and collided with a running Bert Porlock.

'Whatever is happening, Porlock, who is making that dreadful noise?' She was authoritative and severe.

Bert Porlock pulled off his cap and said breathlessly, 'It's Miss Batty, Mum, she's gorn batty.'

'Gorn batty?' queried Miss Amelia in a higher but still aloof tone of voice.

'Yes'm, Miss Myrtle Batty, Mum, the schoolteacher, Mum. She's gorn dotty, crackers.' Poor Bert couldn't seem to make Miss Amelia understand. 'I'm orff for the doctor.' He was relieved to get away. Some of these toffs embarrassed him. He was sure he talked plainer than the country folk, plainer even than the gentry, yet they couldn't understand him always or pretended not to, he thought bitterly. He wondered if they were trying to put him down because he'd come from London (he'd married Polly Bright's friend Kitty Palmer whom he had met while she was in service in London). 'Rotten snobs, some of 'em. I'm not touching me forelock like some of 'em do dahn 'ere.'

Amelia hurried to the study. 'Porlock tells me . . . ,' she began, then ran to her brother's aid. Mrs Gooch was on one side of the occupant of the chair, her brother on the other. The housekeeper and Absalom were both somewhat dishevelled but hardly more so than Miss Myrtle Batty. Her hair was an untidy mess as though giant fingers had torn it assunder, her frock up above her knees, one sleeve hanging out. Her eyes were rolling and Amelia almost put her hands over her ears for the words issuing from Miss Batty's mouth were too vile to hear.

Porlock, she felt, had put it succinctly. Miss Batty had gorn batty, crackers, dotty. Amelia could see that the teacher *was* mad. The poor woman was still struggling, and Amelia wished Porlock had stayed for Absalom and old Mrs Gooch certainly could not hold the wretched creature. Amelia whipped off the belt of her dress and put it round Miss Batty's shoulders and tied it behind the chair. Miss Batty struggled harder and the belt went up round her neck.

'You'll strangle her, Amelia,' shouted Absalom.

'Best thing too,' was Amelia's silent response. As she was struggling to untie the belt, Miss Batty gave a fierce kick and poor old Mrs Gooch fell, knocking her head on Absalom's desk, and landed on the floor.

'Oh dear,' wailed Absalom, and leaving go of the

teacher for a moment, he bent down to help Mrs Gooch, whereupon with another mighty kick he was propelled on top of the poor housekeeper.

Miss Batty must have scored a bulls-eye for poor Absalom was groaning with pain. Amelia looked at the fire-irons and was deciding that perhaps the best first aid was a clout with the heavy brass poker. Fortunately, before Amelia put her desperate remedy into practice, Boxer, the Rectory gardener and odd-job man, burst in. With a clown's eye he took in the scene.

'Vicar and old Mrs Gooch rolling ont' floor. Miss Amelia, brass poker in'er 'and, looked as though she'd already done for vicar and old Mrs Gooch. Miss Batty screaming 'cos she seed what Miss Amelia was a 'goin' to do for 'er.' This would be his tale for his cronies at the White Horse, and for his brother, Stony Plumb, Polly Bright's neighbour and friend.

He went to Miss Batty and sat on her lap. The room seemed suddenly silent. Even the schoolteacher was quiet when the doctor rushed in with Bert Porlock. Boxer rose and stood deferentially to one side. He felt important. He would be needed again. But he was ordered to take Mrs Gooch to the kitchen and give her a glass of water. The doctor would see to her later.

'Water!' He was disgusted. Brandy was what they all needed. Well, he and Mrs Gooch at least.

The doctor quietened Miss Batty with something from a bottle and he and Porlock took her off.

'I'll be back later if you need me, Fox,' he threw over his shoulder to Absalom. Amelia brought Absalom some brandy and poured herself a little.

'Why on earth did Porlock have to bring the wretched creature here?'

Absalom, revived by the brandy was indignant. 'Because, not only am I the rector, Amelia, I am also a

9

guardian of the children's welfare and most importantly, a school governor.'

Amelia would have liked to have said that, with all these responsibilities and with a pure heart, her brother still did not possess the strength of ten men as Porlock and Boxer had displayed.

'Which reminds me,' added Absalom. 'I must see about a replacement for the school immediately. Heaven knows what I shall do tomorrow. There's no one, absolutely no one I can think of in the meantime.'

He looked so wretched that on the spur of the moment Amelia said, 'I'll take the children until the new teacher arrives, if you promise to get her as soon as possible.'

The next morning the children sat in school awaiting their new taskmaster, whoever it might be, the boys too apathetic to tease the girls. What had they to look forward to but another Miss Batty? The first thing a new teacher would do would be to remove the cane from the cupboard and place it on her desk, then gaze round the room looking for future delinquents.

It was freezing cold in the unheated room. It always was in the mornings and the children fidgeted with painful chillblains and cuffed their running, red noses. Miss Batty always stayed in her outdoor clothes and mittens until one of the boys had been delegated to fetch wood and coke to light the stove. No boy would have dared take this task upon himself until ordered to do so by Miss Batty.

The door opened. In walked the Reverend Absalom Fox followed by his sister, Miss Amelia Fox. Mr Jonas Paine, the undertaker, brought up the rear, in his hands his shiny top hat with its wide chiffon band and flowing ends.

'Oh dear,' said Miss Fox, shivering visibly. 'It's

absolutely freezing in here. Could one of you boys light the stove, please?' Her voice was the voice of authority, staccato, severe. 'And you children had better put on your coats until the room is less chill.' The words belied the tone. *'Could'* and *'Please!'* Miss Batty always said, *'YOU,* light the stove and be quick about it, and I want no noise.' And 'Coats!' Coats in school – it was unheard of. Amelia was surprised there was no concerted rush for coats.

When all was quiet, the rector spoke. He appeared somewhat uncomfortable as though he did not relish his task and wanted to get it over as quickly as possible and be off to more pleasurable pursuits. Not a strong character but a kindly man; the predominance of poverty among the children embarrassed him.

He told them he hoped their new teacher would arrive any day now, a Miss Arabella Fish. In the meantime his dear sister, he nodded towards Amelia, would be with them. He hoped they would be good children, for Miss Amelia would continue to guide them in the ways of the church so that they would become God-fearing people, and live their lives with deep humility, content in the estate in which it had pleased Almighty God to deliver them.

Wheel and Wally, Polly's twins, who had been successful in winning the job of stove-lighting, now banged down the top of the stove with an almighty crash. The Revd Absalom sat down.

Mr Jonas Paine now came forward. He was present in his capacity as a senior member of the church council. He was the only one who was interested really. He liked ceremonies. He liked to impress people as well as bury them. He thought he had realised his ambition in life by becoming an undertaker. Had he but known it, he was, by nature, a failed actor, bard,

11

preacher. In his solemn workshop he composed speeches for burials, poems for the bereaved and epitaphs for the tombstones. He knew his was the oratory which gave the bereaved the strength to carry on. Chief mourner, he played the part even off duty; well, he was never off duty, being dressed always in sombre black.

Jonas began by not only repeating word for word what his rector had said, albeit in more mournful tones, but he carried on with an oration of his own.

'Good heavens,' thought Amelia, 'Whose demise is he celebrating now? We might just as well be up at the churchyard.' The word 'celebrating' amused her, and looking round the room at the children she was very surprised. 'I do believe they are thinking as I am.' An imp of mischief entered her soul. Drawing from her pocket a large white handkerchief she blew her nose with such intensity (this gift of Amelia's had always irritated her mother intensely) as to drown Jonas's mournful monologue. For a moment he forgot his next words and with perfect timing Amelia stood up.

'I am sure the children would wish to thank the rector and Mr Jonas Paine for coming here today and also for their kind thoughts and words.' She led the children in applauding the defeated and departing males. Something very peculiar had happened to Amelia in that cold and repelling classroom. Chilly and bored listening to her brother, she had been regretting her impetuous offer to carry on for the time being. She had nothing in common with children, was not even sure she liked them.

It had happened at the end of her brother's speech. She had heard the words all her life, the same sentiment contained in her father's favourite hymn:

> The rich man in his castle

12

The poor man at his gate,
He makes them high or lowly
And orders their estate.

She had looked at the children and for the first time actually thought about the words of the hymn. Was this why most of them looked thin and poor and cold? Why did they not all rush at her invitation to don outdoor clothes? Was it possible some of them had no such possessions? She lifted the lid of the stove and threw in some more wood and coke. Well, she'd start off by having a warm classroom.

She called the register. She looked round the room. Surely she should have more pupils than this? Education in 1903 was free.

'Where is . . . ?'

'Please, Miss, he's a "stone pickin".'

'Please, Miss, 'er mam's 'aving a baby.'

'Please, Miss, 'es up the farm.'

And so it went on. Children sorely needed at home. Children doing the work of men and women. Children receiving no education.

'Please, Miss, he ain't got no boots.'

At the end of her first day at school she was shocked and ashamed.

'Here am I, a woman nearing my twenties, sister of the rector, daughter of a dean, a member of a very Christian family, yet I had not the first awareness really of how the lower classes lived.'

That night at dinner the rich food stuck in her throat. Something must be done. Absalom must help. She tackled him in his study. Like many shy and sensitive people, Absalom felt the deprivations Amelia listed – labouring hard and long hours; lack of education, food and privileges; and the jobs which must be done by the children, stone-picking, baby/mother minding; all this

13

human degradation was in some measure criticism of him as a man and a priest. He was glad she had come into his study with her complaints (and indeed they sounded tragic as she listed them) before he'd taken the Burgundy from the chiffonier, although he needed such sustenance now more than ever. He couldn't tell her he knew of the conditions she was so worked up about for she would have then demanded, 'And what are you doing about it?' Shades of his father!

Was Amelia going to become like their father? He was ashamed at this thought. Amelia had more love and compassion in her little finger than the Dean had had in his whole body. She was a determined organiser, that was all.

He blustered: 'I know all you say is true, Amelia, but I am generous with gifts of money to the poor at Christmas, and I do arrange for Mrs Gooch to prepare parcels of food for the destitute.'

'Though I give my money to the poor and have not charity . . .,' Amelia began. Then she saw Absalom look at the fireplace and then flinchingly at her. 'What's the matter, have you lost something?'

'No, Amelia, I was just thinking of Miss Batty.'

Amelia exploded. 'So you think I am going to become like that poor creature?' She was silent for a moment then laughed merrily. 'You are afraid I shall attack you with the poker, oh brother!' She came behind him and put her arms round his shoulders, resting her face on his head. 'Darling boy, I know you are the most generous of men and everyone loves you. You are the best rector they've ever had. I am not criticising you. I want us to alter things at the roots.'

Absalom was relieved but he wished Amelia wouldn't show her affection like this; suppose Mrs Gooch came in. It was all right for a wife but not a

14

sister. Yes, he would like that. He went off for a moment into a dream world where a gentle sweet creature would share his study, his bed and his life with him, one who was not a firecracker like Amelia.

Amelia tapped his face. 'You're dreaming again. Now let's be practical. By the way, I was looking up the meaning of names today. Yours is most applicable to the present situation. Absalom means Man of Peace; your second name Gerald means Fighter, Man with Spear. I recall mother was very pleased she had insisted on choosing your second name; she detested your first name which she said was Hebrew. Now I am wondering whether she was having a sly joke on father; certainly he could never have known what Gerald meant. I know he loathed it, thinking it foppish, but I suppose in the first flush of marriage even he might have been a little tender with his wife.'

'And what does your name mean?' Absalom was now a little irritable.

'Oh, I'm all right in that direction. I'm just plain Amelia, struggling or labouring, and I shall be doing a lot of that from now on.'

'I must have a few moments to think now, Amelia. I have the parish council meeting in half an hour.'

'Then go wield your spear, Gerald.' Amelia stood up and waved an invisible spear.

'I shall need more than a spear. Don't forget I have Squire Wilton and Colonel Southaby to contend with, two real diehards.' He picked up the metal firescreen and held it in front of him. 'My shield?' They both laughed loudly.

Amelia said, 'Let's have some wine.' Reaching for the bottle she tripped over the rug. Absalom dropped his 'shield' with a clatter to pick her up and they both collapsed helpless with laughter.

15

Old Mrs Gooch hearing the noise rushed to the study and put her head round the door. She hadn't got over the Miss Batty incident and when she saw the reverend and Miss Amelia on the floor, the fireplace in disarray and Miss Amelia with a bottle of wine in her hand she closed the door and went away. It was all too much for her and she told Ernest her cat about it. Amelia hadn't seen Mrs Gooch peering round the door and she went off to the kitchen for some biscuits. She paused in the passage as she heard Mrs Gooch's mumbled monologue to the cat and then returned to Absalom.

'Mrs Gooch is beginning to behave very strangely. I am wondering if we should engage younger domestics?'

Absalom held up his hands in mock horror. 'Hold on, Amelia, one step at a time. Mrs Gooch will be good for some years, I am sure of that.'

Amelia was silent. Well it didn't really matter to her anyway; she would be gone when Miss Arabella Fish arrived any day.

Alas, Miss Arabella Fish did not arrive and indeed would never arrive. She was willing (too willing according to the Bishop) but the authorities were adamant in their rejection of the lady. Absalom informed his sister that Miss Fish would not be coming to their school because, according to the Bishop, she had been found in the most compromising manner by, of all people, the vicar of her parish church.

Miss Fish was, or had been, the village schoolmistress at a hamlet some miles from Great Little Tisbury. She had married secretly a widower from a neighbouring village. They were short of money, her parish council frowned on married women as teachers, and she had applied for the post at Great Little Tisbury where she understood no such ban applied and, what was most important, there was an empty cottage next door to the school.

Her husband had visited her one day after school and because of their rare meetings with one another and because she lived in lodgings, the privacy of the school cloakroom was an ideal nuptial chamber for the newly weds. In a world of passion, in a world of their own, they thought, sure that the door was locked, they were far away when they were rudely interrupted by the vicar. He had been passing the school and, pausing for a moment deep in thought, and having acute hearing, he heard strange sounds wafting through the window of the cloakroom. Deciding to investigate, knowing the school would be empty at this time of day, he crept round the back of the building, collecting on the way a stout cudgel with which to attack an intruder. He came upon a sight so shocking that for a moment he was transfixed.

On the floor of the cloakroom was what he could only describe as a writhing mass of bare legs. When he was able to focus he saw that there were four legs, the bare legs round the waist of the owner of one pair of legs were female legs, the second pair of legs which seemed to match each other were hairy and therefore male. Then the owner of the female legs surfaced her head from around the body on top of her. Miss Arabella Fish! Now the head belonging to hairy legs also turned in his direction. The eyes looked fierce and strange and somewhat feverish.

The vicar staggered back as Miss Arabella Fish let out a blood-curdling scream. The vicar had raised his cudgel at the ready as he had entered the room and Miss Arabella Fish was fearful on which part of her anatomy, or worse still her lover's, the cudgel would fall. She needn't have feared, the vicar turned away from the scene with great difficulty and left the school. He staggered across to his Vicarage where his wife was entertaining the Mothers' Union. They were having tea and biscuits.

He burst into the drawing-room, cudgel still in hand. It would have been appropriate had he shouted, 'Out, out, the Philistines are upon us,' but, trying to be calm, he said, 'Ladies, may I ask you to adjourn. Something extremely important has come up. I must have a discussion with my wife immediately.'

The ladies left, hazarding guesses as to what was so important that it could deprive them of their tea and biscuits. The vicar's wife closed the door on the departing ladies and called 'Algernon.' He wasn't downstairs. She was very puzzled and somewhat intrigued. Algernon had never discussed anything important or urgent with her before.

She traced him to their bedroom. He was in bed.

'Aren't you well?' she enquired in a wifely manner.

He raised his head. 'Lock the door.'

She locked the door. She looked out of the window. Was someone following her husband, someone from his past? She was a great reader of novelettes, secretly resting one open, inside their large Bible, so that an unexpected visitor catching her unawares would think her a pious reader of the scriptures. No, there could be nothing like that, her husband's life was an open book, albeit dull, extremely dull.

'Draw the curtains,' hissed Algernon. When the door was locked, the curtains drawn, she approached the bed to enquire as to the mystery, when, to her amazement, although she didn't have much time to think, a naked Algernon leapt from the bed felling her to the floor. He literally tore her clothes from her; a bit impatient he grew here for her whalebone corsets were always difficult to unlace, even for her, she who had laced and tied them every day of her adult life. At long last came the rape of the vicar's wife. Perhaps it could hardly be called rape for the vicar's wife was a passionate woman and, until now, an unsatisfied one. She loved the tales of masterly, almost brutal men, and, oh, sheikhs in the desert.

'My sheikh,' she cried as Algernon assaulted her body. Fortunately she was a physically strong woman and when the battle was over and the triumph won, she it was who respectably dressed, went with jaunty steps to the kitchen and ordered 'Tea for two'. Sheikh Algernon hardly had strength to crawl to his bed where he slept through the night naked and (although not satisfied) ashamed.

The next morning he journeyed to convey to the Bishop the failings of Miss Arabella Fish, which were too shocking to be transposed to paper. The Bishop, in turn, set the wheels in motion for the dismissal of Miss Fish and advised Absalom of her unsuitability for the post at his school. It was futile for Miss Fish to show her marriage lines. Such behaviour would have been out of place (according to the vicar) in the sanctity of the marriage bed. The vicar's wife was sad that her husband took this attitude, which she thought smacked of hypocrisy, but as long as he retained his passionate mastery in their marriage bed, what did hypocrisy matter?

Miss Amelia was intrigued when she received half the news from Absalom. Only half, and that watered down. He had pure principles where the finer feelings of ladies were concerned. He was dismayed when Amelia appeared unusually interested. She liked to hear about people who were brave enough to be

19

different. To be honest, they were much more likeable and a greater joy to be with than the pillars of the church, or even society.

Amelia said she would leave college until the following year and get the village school into good shape and running order for a new teacher. Many battles did she wage with the council, the locals, the Bishop, but loyally supported by her dear brother, her strength of purpose and the knowledge she was in the right gradually won over most of the opposition and the school became a focal point of the village, and Miss Amelia Fox a much loved member of the community.

If she dreamed of college for herself these days, no one ever knew, her sights were set on high places for her children. She was busy and loving every minute of it so that it came as a great surprise to her when Thomas Bright asked if his little sister Jet might come to school. He had, he said, taught the little girl to read and write.

'Jet!' Amelia was more than surprised. Surely Mrs Bright hadn't had another child. Or was there a child she hadn't seen when she visited? 'What about Bridget? She must be nearly four. Of course, I was thinking about a birthday present for her the other day.'

Thomas smiled. 'Bridget insists she's Jet, Miss Amelia, and we all call her Jet. I don't think she'll like to go back to being called Bridget.'

'Jet?' Amelia was relieved Jet was Bridget. 'I think Jet Bright is lovely and I shall look forward to entering her name in the register on Monday next.'

Amelia knew personally the home circumstances of all her children and thus was able to help where it was needed. She employed lunch-time help and had persuaded the parish council to build a kitchen on to

20

the back of the school.

Over at the Rectory there was now a young strong lad, Saul, to help Boxer Plumb in the garden so that in the winter there were vegetables for the hot soup the children had at lunch and in the summer salads, and fruit. The lunches were simple: soup, potatoes in their jackets in winter, lettuce, cheese and fruit in the summer with bread. Simple meals, easy meals to prepare but luxury to the majority of the children.

Although Amelia was godmother to little Jet Bright she really didn't know much about the children's father or how they came to be living at the Dower House and why Judith Bright, the comfortably-off widow, should favour the one grandchild, Judy, whereas Sarah Hilton, their maternal grandmother, loved and was loved by all Polly's children.

Amelia decided to call on Polly to confirm that little Jet would be coming to school. Amelia had other children of three years of age but in *their* circumstances these little ones would be better off at school. Perhaps Polly had a job where she could no longer take Jet, or was it, as Thomas had said, that little Jet was very forward for her age?

Amelia couldn't have timed her visit better. The children were down in the village with their grandmother Hilton, The Plumbs were visiting friends and would collect the children and bring them home in the evening, so Polly was alone and in a worried mood. She was quite happy for Jet to go to school for then she could work full time on the farm or elsewhere, but she realised with her last child a baby no longer they were all growing up. The years were passing; one day she would have to tell Thomas of his birth and parentage and Jet about her father.

Jet's father, Hugh Neale, was now in Canada and

sent money from time to time. Physically his wife remained well and although Polly had hoped she and Hugh would be together by the time their daughter was old enough to understand things, she couldn't see this happening. In any case Polly wouldn't want her release from worry at the expense of Hugh's poor dear wife who had been stricken mentally and had done no one a bad turn during her short time of happiness before she became ill.

Polly was sometimes frantic at the thought of telling Thomas about the past. Hugh, had he been here, would have helped in that respect too; the children had loved Uncle Hugh, although it was only natural their memories of him should be growing dim, even though Polly always read little bits of his letters to them.

'What I need, what I've always needed, is a friend of my own age,' thought Polly. She couldn't have had a better friend in life than Mrs Plumb but she could see herself left with the dreadful ordeal of telling her children how she had wronged them really, for Mrs P was much older than Polly.

Amelia, arriving while she was in this worried state, was the means of opening the floodgates of the past for her. The two ladies, from different worlds, sat sipping tea and eating cake. Amelia learnt that afternoon all she had wanted to know about Polly and her family.

Polly had lived at the Dower House since she was 13 when she had gone into service with the eccentric elderly mother of the master at the Hall, Lady Margaret Brensham. Her son had been killed in a mountaineering accident and, disliking her daughter-in-law, she had taken up residence at what she called the Dower House. She installed Stony Plumb and Mrs P in the little cottage and Polly in the Dower House with her. These three looked after her needs. Polly worked hard and was happy, although it was not much of a life for a young girl. She thought she was very lucky to have obtained such a good situation.

The master's widow spent most of her life in town letting out the shooting and the Hall from time to time. She had one son, Dominic, a boy of Polly's age and until he went away to school he spent much of his time at his grandmother's. He and Polly, two young things, were thrown together in this strange household.

Here it became awkward for Polly to continue. It was getting dark and she said she must light the lamps.

'No Polly,' said Amelia, already moved by Polly's reminiscences and sensing there was still some worry on Polly's mind. 'Let's sit in the firelight for a little while longer. It is very peaceful here in this house I find. If there is anything I can ever help you with do trust me, I beg you.'

The words, sincerely and warmly meant, Polly was sure were the final key to the breakthrough Amelia made that afternoon. In the dark firelit room she learned of Thomas's conception and of Jet's miracle birth. She took Polly's hands at the end of the story and assured her that if she ever needed help she would always be there. She was honoured by Polly's confidence in her.

'I have never had a friend of my very own, Polly. Will you be that friend?'

'Oh Miss Ameelee,' blurted Polly, and both women laughed. Polly lit the lamps and made more tea and Amelia told Polly of her early life. Polly said she hoped she would have the honour to be godmother to Miss Ameelee's firstborn, which sent Amelia back to the Rectory smiling.

Amelia was very pleased she had gone to see Polly. She felt she could tell Polly or talk to her about anything. Although she knew Polly had had a hard life, and a sad one, perhaps yet it had been full. She had six lovely children; she was loved too. She could see why Hugh Neale had fallen in love with her. Polly, simple yet wise; Polly, warm and lovely, the starry eyes, the bright copper hair, tall, strong, wanting everyone to be happy, unable to hurt anyone, even loving dearly her employer. It gave Amelia much food for thought.

When she was little and toddled away from the other children Jet always stopped at the bend in the lane. Even when she was grown up and knew that WHAT was beyond the bend was no different from anything around other bends, her mind and thoughts seemed always to stop there. An invisible caution, an unseen barrier, but to what?

Past the bend was 'upalong' to the villagers. Anything over three miles round the turn of the lane was 'upalong'. A distance of over about eight miles was almost foreign parts.

But this morning Jet would be going towards the village, the other way from the bend in the lane where they need never go for everything the Brights needed was in the opposite direction.

All the Brights were walking together on this balmy spring morning. Polly, Thomas, Meg, Judy, Wheel and Wally the twins, and Jet. All accompanying Jet on her first morning at school. Well they would all have been going anyway, except for their mother, but not together. Meg would have hurried ahead to the cross roads to meet her bosom friend Bessie, daughter of Bert Porlock, the carrier, and his wife Kitty. Bessie was the same age as Meg, another fat, placid pudding of a girl. Heads together, arms entwined, straight to school, nothing delaying their progress.

24

Sometimes Judy walked with Thomas, sometimes by herself, but Judy was joined by boys and girls of her own age when nearing the school, glossy blue-black hair, greenish-bluish eyes which could flash anger or disapproval. She neither sought nor rejected this popularity. It was as though she hadn't noticed it. She was her own 'woman'; she knew what she wanted and was quite sure she would obtain it.

It was always surprising that the twins ever reached school; there was so much to distract them on the way. Birds' nests, rabbit holes, games to play, friends to collect. Judy ignored the twins or lost her temper with them. They amused Thomas and he envied them their healthy appetites and excited absorption and approval of the world around them. He envied them their twin-ship and thought them very fortunate.

And Thomas? Polly's firstborn. An adult from birth, it seemed to Polly. He'd never been any bother, and sometimes Polly felt Thomas was even older than his mother. A studious boy, thoughtful of others, respected by others, loved by all his family. He'd been Judy's special property, or so she thought, until Jet was born, and now it seemed to Judy that there was an attachment between Thomas and Jet which was like cement, never to be broken.

At first Judy thought it was because Jet was a baby and everyone makes a special fuss of babies, but as Jet began to grow up it was obvious she was one of those grown-up children like her brother Thomas was. Although they looked so different – Thomas fair and Jet copper-coloured like their mother – they under-stood each other and sometimes Judy thought she caught a secret smile passing between the two of them.

'It's only natural you'd be a bit jealous, Judy, but she's only a baby. Thomas had to look after her when

25

she was first born and I was poorly. He loves you just as much as he always did, he doesn't love the baby more'n you.' Polly would comb and brush Judy's hair, trying to soothe the jealous monster away. She tried to be patient but it was difficult. Polly wasn't of a jealous nature herself but she could understand a little Judy's outbursts.

She had been pleased that Thomas was so good with Jet. It made life easier when she'd had to go to work. She sighed. 'Poor Judy, just like her grandmother, Judith Bright. Still, no one'll take advantage of our Judy, that's for sure.'

This morning they all walked together. Jet was given piggy-backs and lifts in turn by Polly, Thomas, Meg and the twins. Judy refused to give Jet a chair lift with Meg. 'My arm hurts', was her excuse. Jet was glad, not because Judy's arm hurt, but that she wasn't going to have a lift from Judy. She'd probably have dropped her and then grumbled because Jet cried.

Judy couldn't stand cry-babies, which made Jet all the more tearful. But this morning Judy had given Jet a new hair ribbon Grandmother Bright had bought her. This pleased Polly, Thomas and Jet, and Judy was bathed in their approbation.

'Perhaps she'll be a bit happier when she grows up,' was her compliment to Jet.

'Oh yes, course she will,' agreed Polly, 'She'm only a little one really even though she is going to school.'

Jet looked back at the house. She didn't want to leave it. It would be lonely with no one in it. Perhaps Stony would be going along to see what he could do with the garden. He would come to dig and hoe and weed and try to get some semblance of order into what he called a 'proper turbillan patch'.

Jet would follow Stony into the garden to listen to his

first words and watch his face. The ritual was always the same. He'd plunge his fork into the ground. He'd then turn in a circle, survey the garden, hold his back, straighten up as though in great pain or his back giving way, and in a mournful voice he'd say, 'Oh pray, oh pray'. He'd then commence his gargantuan task and utter not another word all day. Indeed, except for his gardening pleas to the Lord, Jet had never heard Stony talk about anything except his ferrets.

She hated Stony's ferrets. She shuddered when they looked at her with their strange pink eyes, ever fearful they would take her for a rabbit or such like. Her mother had made her a little fur hat but whenever she passed Stony's cottage she took it off and stuffed it up her frock. Stony's ferrets were Fred, Flossie, Flo and Phil because Stony wanted all their names to begin with the sound of 'f'.

Stony and his wife, Mrs P, had no children. The ferrets were Stony's children and the cats were Mrs P's children. Jet loved the two well-fed black glossy creatures. They purred like thunder. Tibby had a little bit of white fur on his chest. Mrs P had had them both 'seen to' to keep them at home.

Except for the ferrets, and they were in a shed outside, Jet loved everything about Stony and Mrs P. Their dear little white cottage. About fifteen yards from Jet's house, it looked as though it could have tumbled off the side and had been left just as it came to rest. Mrs P told fortunes. Everything she saw in the cards or the teacups came true. Everybody knew this, except of course Judy who tossed her lovely black hair and said, 'Well I don't believe it and I aint scared.' Judy wouldn't tell what Mrs P had told her; 'Mind yer own business,' she would say.

'I expect Plumb will miss me now I'm growed up and

27

gone to school.' Jet decided to do a drawing of Tibby and Toby for Mrs P. She would surprise Miss Ameelee too for Thomas said she would do drawing at school. He said it was lovely there now and Judy said, 'Trust *her* not to have had Miss Batty, like we did.'

There was no one else at home to miss her, for the rest of her cousins and uncles and aunts were near the village. Uncle Dan'l, once a ship's carpenter, now had a woodwork shop in the village. Uncle Albert and Auntie Bella had a general store but Uncle Joseph and Aunt Emma were 'up the Hall'. Jet wasn't fond of Uncle Joseph and Aunt Emma. He was the game-keeper.

Once when Jet was visiting Granny Hilton, Uncle Joseph had come to see his mother. Aunt Emma was with him and Jet's three girl cousins Emma, Harriet and Maud. They looked like Aunt Emma except they didn't wear that lace around their necks, the lace with bones in it, but they were just as stiff and as thin as Aunt Emma. Jet smiled hallo to her cousins. Three tongues poked out in unison at her and just when Jet was poking out her tongue in return Aunt Emma turned round and saw her. She drew her daughters away from Jet and when Granny Hilton saw them to the door Aunt Emma said, 'You were too easy with Polly. It's Thomas and Bridget I feel sorry for when they find out.' Jet heard no more and when Granny Hilton came back she looked cross.

'Let's make some fresh tea, and I'm blowed if I doan't cut me saffron cake. I wouldn't cut it for *that* one.' Cake on a Friday! Granny gave Jet a piece to take home with her. She was looking forward to giving it to Thomas for it was his favourite cake. She got Gran some water from the pump for Gran wouldn't ask Uncle Joseph or Aunt Emma to get any for her. She had a tiny little bucket which she kept especially for Jet's young arms.

'Soppy cat,' said Judy when Jet insisted on turning round and waving goodbye to the house and telling it she'd be home again after school. Jet loved the house and knew the house loved her. It was white and beautiful. She knew her mother was a caretaker but wasn't sure what that was, except it made it their home.

Thomas had the two large attics at the top of the house and he'd let Jet sit in the dormer windows. Marvellous views right across the trees to the Hall. The old lady who'd lived in the house had loved the copper beech and had had all the hedges cleared so that the tree was alone in splendid space. It was at the bend in the lane that the hedges grew thick and tall obscuring what was beyond, making it frightening for the young and imaginative Jet.

As they reached the village school, a red-bricked, one-storey building, Polly gave Jet a last inspection. The others ran on ahead into the playground. Polly straightened Jet's ribbon – she was wearing it in a bandeau to keep her thick glossy hair tidy.

'Now be a good girl Jet. You're grown up now.'

Polly poked her head into the schoolroom and spoke to someone Jet couldn't see.

'I've brought Jet, I mean Bridget. Shall I leave her in the playground? I'm off to Bowman's Farm; they need help in the dairy.'

Jet couldn't hear any reply but Polly opened the door wide, pushed Jet inside and said, 'You be good now,' and was gone. Miss Amelia was sitting at her desk and gazed at her new pupil. Buttoned boots, black stockings, long grey worsted woollen frock, starched white pinafore on the front of which was pinned a white

29

cambric square, the pupil's handkerchief, sign of respectability and a good home!

No different from other well-cared-for pupils, poor but clean, of the village school. Such a serious little girl, thought Amelia, looking at the straight nose, firm mouth and large grey eyes, unsmiling and watchful at the moment.

It was the hair which struck an incongrous note in all this adult seriousness in one so young. Bright, flaming, shining copper, long, tamed by a luxurious ribbon, not seen on one of Amelia's pupils normally. Wide, rainbow satin. 'What a beautiful satin ribbon, Bridget, or shall we call you Jet, as your mother tells me you prefer that to Bridget?'

Amelia wasn't prepared for the vivid smile which transformed the serious almost solemn little face.

'Judy gave it to me, she's my sister, and I like to be Jet.' There was a pause then suddenly a large sigh came from the little girl. 'Thank you, Miss Ameelee,' she said. Amelia smiled, stood up and took Jet's hand.

'Let me see, I think you would like this little pink chair at the table with Jinny Porlock. She started some weeks ago and she will be able to show you what to do for the moment.'

Miss Amelia went to the door, rang a bell and after a few minutes' silence the children came in and sat at their various desks. Jet thought she'd never seen so many children before. She felt quite excited to be one of their number. She liked Jinny Porlock too for she was just like Meg's friend Bessie, Jinny's big sister, except that Bessie was bigger. There were twin boys on Jet's table too, Auntie Bella's boys Albert and Frederick. Thomas looked across the room and caught Jet's eye. They smiled at each other and Thomas was content. Jet was happy at school.

30

Jet had seen the village school before she became a pupil there. She'd seen it over her shoulder when she came into the village on quarter days with her mother. She'd had to look over her shoulder at the village school because it was behind a row of larch trees over a little bridge on the side of the road leading into the village. A low, red-bricked building with a miniature clock tower in white painted wood.

The clock chimed the hours and seemed in a great hurry to finish chiming. Polly said when she went to school it chimed the quarters and halves as well. She thought the birds had choked something up with their nests.

Quarter days were when her mother was solvent again. She didn't go to work at Bowman's Farm on quarter days. Jet went to stay with whoever was available when her mother went to work, but if Mrs P was working, or Granny Hilton, then Jet went to work with her mother. She wasn't keen on this, the farmer and his wife were very kind but they had one dog which was a bit 'sassy' and he seemed jealous of Jet and would snap at her if she moved about much.

On quarter days Jet's mother would sing as she hurried around getting ready for the momentous journey. She always left the place tidy, for then it was so nice to come home to when feet are tired. The fire was damped down, the great black kettle freshly filled on the hob, a last look round, a tug of her hat, a tidying pat to Jet, and 'We're off' her mother would cry.

On quarter days Polly wore a hat, a brown felt one with a glass pin on winter quarter days, and in spring and summer a yellow straw. This was Polly's favourite hat and it had poppies all round the brim. As they went along the country lanes she talked non-stop to Jet, just as though she, Jet, was grown up. The straw hat had been her mother's wedding hat, the poppies removed and a 'floaty' scarf, a piece of her mother's wedding dress, stitched round.

'I stitched it so the stitches never showed.'

Jet thought her mother very clever to sew like this and she wondered where the stitches could have been hidden. Her mother's best brown shoes always squeaked but she only wore them on quarter days for, as her mother said 'They're for high days and holidays'. At home, working about, Polly wore a pair of men's old boots and a floppy sunbonnet when gardening.

Jet learned all about the Lady Margaret her mother had worked for and whose house they lived in. Jet cried when she knew it wasn't their house, but her mother said, 'Silly kate, don't cry when we're out on our day off. Perhaps it *will* be our house one day.' Then her mother stopped and looked sad so Jet stopped crying.

Polly received money from the trustees of Lady Margaret's Will mainly for the upkeep of the house, but here she was lucky for by her brother Daniel, friends Stony and Boxer Plumb, the house was kept in tip-top condition all for the cost of the materials, and often they were free. Polly and her friend Mrs P, like so many women of their class, were practical workers themselves.

Her mother always wore cotton gloves on quarter days. She'd fold them over where they wanted mending and always said, 'Blow it, I mean't to mend these last night; remind me, Jet, when we get home.' Or else she'd laugh and say, 'Now then Jet, did you forget to remind me?'

Jet knew that the lady of the Dower House had lost her husband and her son in accidents, and Polly told her, 'My children's father was lost at sea, Jet; it's a cruel world.' But even these memories couldn't stem

32

the feeling of excitement which emanated from her mother on quarter days. It was as though Polly wanted her to know all the sad things at a happy time.

When they reached the village, and Jet had seen the school over her shoulder, if the children were in the playground, the noise was unbelievable.

'Just hark at them little beggars,' Polly would say fondly. 'Not long now, Jet, and you'll be along of them.' Jet held her mother's hand tightly; loud noise always worried her.

First of all they went to the grocer's. Uncle Albert Hilton was the grocer and he sold everything. He was older than Uncles Joseph and Daniel but he was jolly like Uncle Dan'l. He had been coachman to a rich bachelor gentleman who had been very modern and bought a motor vehicle. Uncle Albert had learnt to drive and when the gentleman died he left Uncle Albert not only the motor car, which was high up in the air with two seats by the driver, but a small sum of money, so he married Auntie Bella who was parlour-maid for the same gentleman, and they had taken over the shop which had been neglected by the previous owner who had grown very old.

Auntie Bella loved children and had twin boys of Jet's age. Judy had told Jet they weren't really Auntie Bella's babies, they were doctors' babies, for they had been left somewhere in a bag. Jet remembered when Dr Skelton had come to them once he'd forgotten to take his Gladstone bag home with him and Thomas had cycled to the doctor's house with the bag. Old Dr Skelton was very forgetful; perhaps he'd been taking the babies to a mother and the bag had got heavy so he'd given them to Auntie Bella, for the grocer's shop had a tricycle with a square basket on the front to carry heavy things. It was lucky Auntie Bella had no children

33

when the doctor left the twin boys because when people in the village who already had children had another baby people always said, 'Oh poor woman, another mouth to feed.'

If her mother needed cottons or tapes they'd call at Wash's Emporium. This was owned by Miss Emmeline Wash, a tall, angular, dominant female who'd inherited the shop from her father. She'd been trained in millinery, and dressmaking, was eminently capable and served rich and poor of the surrounding villages. Mrs P had been friends with Miss Emmeline's mother, a mouse-like creature under the thumb of first, her husband, the late Josiah Wash, and then her daughter Emmeline, a real chip off the old block.

It had been a village scandal when Mrs Wash had eloped to, not with, her first love, the widowed station-master Eli at the Railway Halt some miles from the village. Mrs P had visited her old friend and told Polly, 'You wouldn't recognise Mrs Wash. She looks years younger. She's as happy as a sandboy, and the three of them (Eli, Mrs Wash and Bill, the old bachelor porter) is like schoolkids together. She mothers them and they fetch and carry for her. She says she was a real silly woman to put up with the life she had for all those years. Emmeline's still not talking to her mother and her mother don't care a fig.'

Jet thought it was a lovely shop. She liked the pincushion on the arm of the young lady assistant and the tape round the neck of the young man. She thought they looked very rich and was impressed when Polly said, 'I wouldn't be surprised if our Judy got to work for Miss Wash, for it's obvious our Judy thinks she's too good for service. Still I'm not worried really. Her grandmother'll see our Judy's all right.' Jet knew her mother didn't mean Granny Hilton. She meant Granny

34

Bright, who looked like Judy a bit, and liked Judy best of all. But the others weren't jealous; they all came in for presents from time to time. Jet knew this wasn't because Granny Bright loved them all but because her mother had said, 'I won't have one fished and the others fowled.' Jet had been to Granny Bright's with Judy once. She remembered the glass cases, tall, rounded tops, with birds, flowers and fruit inside.

'Don't touch,' ordered Grandmother Bright.

'It's all right, Granma. Jet's not like the boys.' Jet remembered Judy championing her. It was only at home Judy could be funny-tempered; she always stuck up for her family when she was away from home.

Judy was braver than Jet could be. She went with Judy in Grandmother Bright's pony and trap. They were off to the blacksmith's, just out of the village, where a pony Granny Bright had bought was being shod. Granny Bright had ridden all her life and Judy was going to have this pony. Judy went right into the forge where the sparks were flying and held the pony's head while it was being shod. Jet could see Granny Bright was very proud of Judy.

'She's a beauty,' Granny Bright said and Jet knew she didn't mean the horse, which Jet could see was truly beautiful but which she refused to give sugar to because it was too lively, kicking it's legs about. It had flowing black hair like Judy.

Jet always visited the butchers with her mother. Mr George Moon, Purveyor of Fine Meat and Game, found Polly a fine prospect. Straw boater on head, snowy white apron tied around his portly waist, waxed moustache sharp as a stiletto at each end. His fat red hands held Polly's longer than it took to take her scribbled order. Mrs Moon, thin, childless, would stand behind the glass-topped door leading from the shop to the parlour, ever suspicious of Polly and Mr Moon. Polly, who had fended off Georgie Moon when he'd been a fat schoolboy in her class, thought it just a little bit of fun, and she did get served exceptionally well for the money she was able to spend. Mr Moon thought there was no other woman like Polly with her coils of bright hair, her dancing blue eyes and her figure, attractive and curvaceous. She was always so happy. He admired her lively spirit, knowing how hard she had to work after the tragic death of her husband.

'There's lots of tradesmen our Poll could be seconds to,' said Stony proudly.

Jet didn't want her mother to be seconds to anyone, especially not Butcher Moon, with his scarlet fat cheeks, his podgy fingers and sharp chopper. He might want to come and live in their house. Oh no, not her house. She would die. She would tell it to get haunted. If she talked to the house she knew it would send at least a ghost to frighten away the large figure of Mr Moon. When he brought anything to the house he'd sit in the kitchen drinking tea. Jet never left the kitchen then to go and play. It was obvious Mr Moon didn't like Jet. 'The way that child stares at a body!'

Polly only ever bought meat on quarter days, and then not very much – shin of beef, marrow bones for the soup she kept permanently bubbling on the stove, and a rib of beef for special occasions or at Christmas an aitchbone of beef which Mrs P and everybody else called an 'edgebone'. Mr Moon often put bones and pieces of meat and offal in Polly's way without charging. He enjoyed the cup of tea and a sit-down in Polly's warm and inviting kitchen.

Polly and the Plumbs kept their own pigs and chickens and a couple of goats. They were able to sell and barter all sorts of things. They smoked, salted, pickled, dried, and nothing was wasted. They made preserves and jams from the fruits around them. Everything was home made, for they set candles, wove material, knitted, sewed, and even made their own soap. Sweet Chestnut, walnut, and almond trees grew in the enormous garden and in the hedgerows nearby hazel nut bushes abounded.

One thing Polly had to buy and which always seemed a big source of worry, children's boots. On quarter days there were boots to be taken or collected from Ernest Endean, the cobbler. His little shop in the village was down three steps from the road. To Jet it was like going down into smelly darkness. The odour of the new leather and the old boots waiting attention made her feel sick.

The cobbler sat with his back to the window. He wore metal-rimmed spectacles, sat always in his short sleeves, small and bowed over the boot he was mending. Sometimes he had a mouthful of nails. Jet was very worried lest he would swallow them, and she kept very still in his shop.

Sometimes as they walked along her mother would look at her, scoop her up and smother her face with kisses.

'Oh Jet, you'm such a serious big-eyed little thing. I could eat you, you're just like . . .', but her mother never ever said who she was like, always either meeting a friend or darting over to look into a garden or a shop. Jet was a bit disapproving of her mother sometimes. She never seemed to mind where she was or who she was with when she would suddenly go off into one of her laughs or jigs.

They would end up their visiting with a call on Uncle Albert and Auntie Bella again. Bread and cheese, pickles, tart and cake, tea and beer, were on the table.

Granny Hilton would come in and a fine time would be had by all. News and gossip, recipes, children, illnesses, everything was discussed. Children were hugged and kissed and invited for holiday stays, then they would be off.

Auntie Bella would take care of the shop while Uncle Albert drove them home with all their goods, except the meat which Butcher Moon would bring up later in the week. Sacks of salt (for preserving), flour, oats, sugar, butter beans, etc. to last Polly and Mrs P to next quarter day. Sometimes Mrs P would come with them on quarter days, then Stony would drive them home.

Tired and happy, they would await the arrival from school of Thomas, Meg, Judy and the twins.

'Did you bring us anything Mam?' Polly always brought them some little surprise, boys' comics from Uncle Daniel, sugar walking-sticks, magazines for Meg and Judy and a large, large bag of pear drops. Often, too, there would be old clothes Granny Hilton had got from the big house where she did cleaning.

Haymaking was a time all the family enjoyed. Polly and the Plumbs earned money and had a fine time at the harvest supper. The older children earned a little pocket money at harvest time stooking the sheaves. They weren't too keen on the gleaning part afterwards but did it because it was so important to get as much corn as they could for the chickens.

It was another time when Jet was a little disapproving of her mother. Her mother worked hard, and Jet and the other children watched from the outer edges of the field as the machine cut the corn and the rabbits and rats ran for cover. Then the snakes. They all looked black as they leapt about at the very centre of the field as though they knew their fate. The men sent in their

38

dogs and followed them with cudgels. It was to Jet a noisy, frightening time. Always hot. Her mother's hair would come tumbling down many times, her frock would be tight across her bosom as she bent and manipulated the fork. She was so deft too at tying up the sheaves. Twelve they'd count out for each stooking. The cider would have flowed freely since lunch time, and Jet thought her mother sang a little louder and laughed a little longer than she had before lunch time. Polly would look at Jet sometimes and say to Mrs P, 'I don't know what I would do without my little guardian.' And after cider time Mrs P would say, 'Jet should have been born the eldest, then Poll.' And they'd both laugh and sometimes dance Jet round in a ring. Then they'd kiss her and say, 'We are only playing, Jetty.' It was all mysterious to Jet.

At the harvest, when Jet had been a schoolgirl for some time, she saw Miss Amelia watching the harvesters. Her mother was laughing and singing and Jet worried what Miss Ameelee would think. But Amelia saw Polly and the workers and envied them their strength and freedom of thought and deed, and their cameraderie.

At one time, all the Brights were at the village school, for mother Polly came to work there. Had the school been run the same as most village schools of that time extra help would not have been needed. Amelia, however, having no experience of teaching elsewhere and now knowing what attending school entailed for children of the local farm labourers, attempted to educate them in a more all-round way. Thus, in addition to the lunch-time food, she gave them lessons in drawing, painting, music, dancing, and extra tuition for bright children. All these extras involved more time and work. But she was determined to give her children all the benefits possible, and with Absalom's support, received permission from the parish for full-time help if the full-time helper would also take on the cleaning. This had been done previously by an elderly villager who was now going to live with a married daughter, so no one was hurt by the change-over.

To Polly it was easier work than she had done previously, for she loved being with the village children. Amelia procured Boxer Plumb's young apprentice Saul to come into school in the morning and light the stove, and clean the boys' outside earth closets, and after school to sweep up. Polly scrubbed the floors at the weekends helped by Meg, Bessie and Mrs P, and other mothers came to help in various ways.

For the first time the parents felt that their children were important to and cared for by someone other than themselves, and the response was all that Amelia had hoped for. She wanted the local community to think of the school as really belonging to them.

She invited local tradespeople to dine at the Rectory, hoping to interest them in the welfare of the school, and among others Miss Wash and Miss Tremlett responded. Miss Wash remembered dancing round the maypole when she was young. She was also something of a pianist and offered to play for the school.

Polly taught the girls cookery and housewifery. Miss Wash took them for singing and, at Judith Bright's request, took Judy for pianoforte. Miss Wash was much taken with Judy. She would make a most superior assistant for her emporium.

Miss Tremlett, the postmistress, wasn't gifted in any one particular way but one afternoon a week she took the children on nature walks. Jet loved this and Miss Tremlett obtained books for her on the strangest subjects connected with the science of nature. And it was through her that others were brought in to help. Her cousin, Alma, who had lived with her husband Timothy Drake in Covent Garden, was a retired elocution teacher, and he a singing teacher. They had been left Pump Cottage, a picturesque house opposite Dr Skelton's ivy-covered Georgian mini-mansion on the outskirts of the village. They had decided to retire to the village where Alma Drake had been born.

'If I know them both,' said an excited Olive Tremlett, 'they will soon get tired of doing nothing. They are such an energetic pair, I am sure they will help us one day when we are ready to perform a play.'

All this voluntary help left Amelia free, with her brother's assistance, to rescue two of her pupils from what would have been a life of dismal depression. Basil Bennett and Eric Simmonds owed their futures to Miss Fox.

Basil was a sleepy boy who just grunted gutturally and ran with tiny steps in a pitched-forward manner. 'Basil, 'e do 'ave the sleeping sickness,' was how he was dismissed by the village. Amelia had spoken to old Dr Skelton about him, and learned that this form of disability was a common occurrence in the villages around. The doctor thought it might be due to cousin marrying cousing so often within the same family. Basil lived with two eccentric old maids who seemed fond of him in the way some people are fond of their pets. Amelia was successful, although it had been hard work, in training Basil to do simple tasks. 'He's harmless enough,' the villagers said.

With Eric it was different. He was a hunchbacked boy with a thin body and a head which looked too large for his frame. He possessed large brown eyes, so dark that they appeared to glitter in the light. He stuttered permanently, and so badly, people had given up even trying to talk to him. Ignored by adults, cruelly teased by the children, his school life was one of abject misery and degradation. Miss Batty had ignored his cruel treatment by the other children which in a way left them free to torment him.

He was the only child of Jacob and Emily Simmonds. Jacob was the night-soil man. Emily had nearly died when Eric was born. People said, 'The Lord should have taken Eric. 'Twould 'ave been a mercy.' But Eric was the only child the Simmonds would have now, and they loved him even more because of his infirmity. They lived some distance out of the village. The night-soil men's pair of tiny cottages were isolated, Eric was the only child in the area, and the Simmonds had no knowledge of his treatment at school.

With the advent of Amelia the teasing of the two children ceased. She was fiercely watchful and was teaching the children to help, if not care for the two disabled lads, 'Future village idiots,' was how the children had regarded Eric and Basil. Amelia discovered that Eric could draw. As a little encouragement for the boy she sent him across to the Rectory to show the Revd Absalom 'your beautiful drawing'. Absalom was at the piano and hadn't seen the boy enter the drawing-room. Eric stood listening to the music and suddenly said, 'Miss said to show you this'. It wasn't until Absalom had admired the drawing that he realised Eric had spoken normally. He asked the boy if he had any other drawings. Eric went into the usual 'convulsions' in an effort to reply, his face scarlet. Then Absalom remembered he had been playing the piano when Eric first spoke. He began to play a little song the children sang in school. 'Will you sing it for me, Eric?' he asked. The little boy sang without stuttering.

That night at dinner the Foxes were quite excited. From then on Eric spent one afternoon each week with Absalom and gradually he began to speak normally, but somewhat rapidly. He could already write because he had always copied from the blackboard but now he was persuaded to read to Absalom, whose gentle patience was rewarded. They were hopeful that one day he would reach the standard of the other children. They had no idea of the shock still in store for them.

One afternoon Absalom was busy with the church accounts, a job he detested – arithmetic was always a bore for him – and the columns gave a different result each time he added up. In disgust he threw the account book on to the table where Eric was reading. Eric looked at the page which had been so exasperating, picked up his slate and chalked the totals on it, passing the slate to Absalom. Slowly the rector checked. Eric's totals were correct. But how could the boy have done such a sum? He was only doing addition and subtraction of two figures at school.

The next day Amelia set special arithmetical problems for Eric which he completed swiftly and correctly. A phenomenon! What could be done? They'd not experienced before, or ever heard of this type of brain, and certainly not one housed in the head of a country lad, a bit of a hunchback, to boot.

Absalom went to see his Bishop, whose brother was a specialist at a London hospital. The Bishop promised to mention Eric's case when he was next in touch with his brother. The months went by, during which time the Foxes gave Eric special tuition. Then, when they had almost given up hope of help from the Bishop's medical brother and were deciding what further they could do to enable Eric to achieve his true potential, they heard that the specialist, holidaying with the

43

Bishop in the country, would visit the school.

Rupert Hartington-Bols was excitedly interested after examining Eric. Mr and Mrs Simmonds allowed him to go to the hospital in Oxford where the specialist was working with an eminent colleague. Eric was to stay with a retired nurse and attend the hospital daily.

Absalom took the Simmonds to Oxford to meet Mrs Holmes, the kindly nurse in whose house it was thought Eric would be living for three to four years. Eric was excited at the conversations he had with educated men and women. They came back to their village with mixed emotions; sad, they were leaving their only child, happy that he would now have a full life. Resigned, realising that in one way they had lost him from their lives but grateful to the Foxes for giving their son opportunity for a better life.

'You have been a missionary in our own land, Amelia,' said Absalom, 'and must feel great satisfaction, but if your self-sacrifice has been hard to bear there is still time for you to think of yourself.'

Amelia smiled. 'Even if I could go to college tomorrow, I could not leave all the unfinished business here. There is Thomas, Jet, and indeed all the children need care. I feel we are in a new era; exciting things are happening, women are emerging from the shadows.'

'Would that there was one for me,' he said wistfully.

Amelia laughed at his sad tone and then was sorry. She patted his arm. 'Perhaps you and I, brother, are destined to walk alone and fill our lives with other people's problems, thus forgetting our single state; and who knows, dear Absalom, which is the most fruitful spiritually?'

Absalom looked mournful and shrugged his shoulders. 'Of course you are right, Amelia; it's just that sometimes I imagine what it would be like to have

44

little ones of my own.'

'I never imagine that for myself,' admitted Amelia. 'But you are comparatively young. I am convinced you will be a family man one day.'

'Oh pray let it be soon.' Absalom put his hands together and Amelia said 'Amen'.

'Naught, naughty,' exclaimed Absalom as Mrs Gooch came in to attend to the fire. They were the strangest rector and sister she had worked for, and she wondered how much longer she could carry on. She was always nervously expecting trouble of some sort ever since Miss Batty was brought in struggling.

'By the way, Amelia, the open scholarship for Dymchester Academy is to be held two weeks next Wednesday. Will you tell Mrs Bright? I will take Thomas, for there is an ecumenical meeting in the morning. I can do some shopping in the afternoon and collect him for home after. So if there is anything you need, make me a list.'

Thomas was the only one concerned who remained calm about the impending scholarship examination. Polly was very worried. She had worked out her money. There was no way, short of a miracle, that Thomas could attend the Academy even if he won the open scholarship. She was cross that she'd allowed herself to be persuaded by Hugh that Thomas should have help because he was clever.

Now in her worried state she imagined Thomas would have been just as happy leaving school at 13 or even 14 and working on the farm. He'd always liked animals and the countryside. She wished she knew now whether he would win the scholarship or not. Should she tell Miss Amelia and the Reverend Absalom now how she felt? She felt cross. Surely they knew Thomas's hopes were just being raised unnecessarily, or didn't

those sort of people know what it cost to keep a child –
and she had six – without a husband's support?

She was so worried she found herself snapping at Jet
and lashing out at the boys. Judy took herself off to her
Grandmother Bright's for a day. This annoyed Polly
too. She knew Judy was loyal to the family but she
couldn't forget her treatment at the hands of her
mother-in-law. She had had to blackmail the lady into
appearing to treat all the children the same by
threatening to keep Judy away from her grandmother.
Polly hadn't wanted to do this, it was against her
nature, but she did it for the other children.

She wondered if Mrs Bright would help if Thomas
needed it but knew immediately that would be the last
straw. Polly wouldn't be able to keep Judy from her
grandmother always.

Jet was worried too. She rushed round after Thomas
fetching things for him. She never mentioned the
scholarship day but Amelia noticed the child was
fretting. She made time to chat to her but there wasn't
much comfort she could give. Jet knew all the
arguments. She could see the difference between
Thomas and his brothers. Amelia discussed Jet with
Absalom.

'She is a gentle, compassionate little soul. Sometimes
I watch her at Sunday School and I wonder if she is not
a little melancholy,' observed Absalom.

'No, no, no.' Amelia was emphatic. 'It's just
that Thomas has taken the place of a father for the
child and he, being the fine character he is, hasn't
helped to dispel her great attachment to him. If Hugh
Neale had been able to stay things might have been
different.'

'I don't know why there is all this depression around.
If Thomas doesn't get the scholarship, as you say things

46

are changing. I am sure we won't allow him to have the most menial of jobs.'

Then Absalom had a letter from Hugh Neale. He knew the scholarship was soon, and also that money would be necessary. He wasn't having too successful a time himself at the moment, and he suggested that either the Reverend or Miss Amelia should remind Polly that the trustees of Lady Margaret's estate might help if Thomas was successful. The application for financial help might come better from someone like the local vicar or teacher.

Amelia wondered why she hadn't thought about Polly's problem of finance before. Of course a son at the Academy would need financial support even though he won free tuition. She knew she would have helped, so would Absalom, but Polly was very proud; she thought she'd had too much outside help already.

Thomas again appeared to be the least worried of all his friends and family on the great day. Jet was up early to see to the kitchen fire. Thomas laughed and said he wished he could enter an examination every day to receive such treatment.

Jet waved him off as he left with Saul in the Foxes' pony trap to pick up the Reverend Absalom. She came back into the house for a moment then rushed off into the garden. Polly followed her. She knew Jet had been sick and felt cross but when Jet turned to come back into the house the sight of the pale, serious face touched her heartstrings.

'Oh Jetty, Jetty, what is Mam going to do with you?'

'It's all right Mam. Let's go to school; the others have gone and I don't want to be late.'

Polly was glad Jet wanted to go to school but felt rebuffed as though she was the child and Jet the mother.

In the evening Jet was in the lane to welcome Thomas home.

'Mrs Livingstone, I presume?' They went into the house laughing. Polly was cooking a meal for the evening. Thomas kissed his mother.

'And now we'll forget all about it, shall we?' He went outside for a minute then returned. 'We are short of kindling, Mam. I'll change my clothes and chop some.'

Polly wondered why they'd all been worried. 'You see?' she said to Jet, and Jet nodded and smiled.

Some time later came the communication signalling Thomas's success. And the trustees were easily persuaded by the Foxes. It seemed that in Lady Margaret's Will there was a loophole which the trustees thought would permit them to agree to an advance being given to Thomas for the purposes of education.

Stony said, 'That wunnerful old soul did it of a purpose. I wouldn't be a bit surprised.'

Boxer said, 'Bright be nachur if not be name,' a joke of his which fell on deaf ears.

'He's a girt fule at times,' apologised Stony, his brother.

It seemed that Thomas's entry to the Academy heralded a number of changes in Great Little Tisbury. Soon after he'd left the village school Meg and her friend Bessie were ready for work. They would be ideal domestic servants and Polly wondered if it was possible for them to obtain situations near to each other, never dreaming that once again the Foxes would prove dear friends to them.

Mrs Gooch had finally left the Rectory. The shock of discovering her missing cat Ernest in a trap, too badly injured to be saved, was the final straw. When Absalom asserted his influence and obtained her a pretty little almshouse, the end one in a row at the edge of the village, and also presented her with a new kitten, she sang the praises of the Reverend and his sister loud and long.

Amelia suggested to Polly and her friend Kitty Porlock that Mrs Gooch's position could be filled by the two girls. She was surprised at their overwhelming gratitude and acceptance for their daughters. It gave her cause for thought again.

'Cor, you wouldn't catch me doing housework in this village,' said a scornful Judy.

'No, I'm goin' to be a hactress,' chorused the twins prancing about the kitchen in mock imitation of their sister. Since the arrival of Alma Drake with her interest in the village school, Judy had been an apt pupil. She spent hours practising strange sounds in front of the mirror.

'That's enough you boys.' Polly rose to her feet but the twins had fled. They never stopped to face Judy when she lost her temper.

'I expect our Judy will be an actress one day, don't you, Mam?' Jet was anxious Judy's temper should evaporate.

'I think there's as much chance of *you* being an actress Jet as there is our Judy, and the sooner she gives up those silly notions and realises she'll have to work for her living like the rest of us, the sooner I'll be pleased.'

Judy was furious. 'Oh it's not big ideas when our Thomas and *her* are told how wonderful they are. Well I'll tell you this, I wouldn't want to be a blooming school marm like she'll be, and I won't go into service, I'll run away first, and Mrs Drake said I've got the voice if I'll work, and Granny Bright's going to pay for lessons for me, and Miss Wash said I'm a quick learner.' Miss Wash was still teaching Judy pianoforte.

Judy went out and slammed the door. 'I don't know what she'll do later on. She wouldn't do dairy work; there's only service. Children are a mixed blessing, Jet, and don't you forget it,' Polly sighed.

But Judy didn't go on a farm or into service a year later. She started as an assistant at Wash's Emporium. Everybody, especially Polly, was much relieved. Grandmother Bright would have liked Judy to have lived with her, but she was sure the work was only temporary, for her beautiful granddaughter would be a fine actress one day, if not famous. It was she who encouraged Judy, and, in Polly's words, 'led her on in her foolishness'.

Before Judy left school Amelia held the first of her Village School Exhibitions. Ambitious, she knew, but in spite of all the things which went wrong it was a great success.

It was held on the last day before the summer holiday. The weather was perfect. Uncle Daniel and Uncle Albert had, with the help of the twins, erected the maypole. Miss Wash was in charge of this.

But first of all the children's school work was on display. To say that the parents were amazed would be an understatement. They were shy and, at first, ill at ease. Amelia wondered if they had come only because her invitation would have appeared as an order to the majority of the parents.

Amelia had opened the school very early, for she knew it was a working day so if the parents came they would come in the morning on the way to the fields, during their short break at noon, or on the way home. The children were let off in the morning for the rest of the day would be a busy one for them.

The bigger children, however, came to help, for

there was much to do; teas to prepare since the school was having sports in the afternoon in the field attached to the buildings; refreshments in the evening for the parents.

It was a festive occasion with bunting and flags. The guest of honour was the Bishop. Well, he was only able to stay for a short time but he was amazed at the transformation Amelia had wrought in the life of the village as well as in the school. People wanted to be part of this new happening. The Bishop had never really liked unfeminine women; they frightened him. They were quicker with their repartee than he could ever be, and the feeling growing in London that women would one day be able to vote terrified him. Yet he had to admit that in Amelia God had made a whole woman. Intelligent, capable, unselfish, and so feminine.

This last description would have amused her. She would have said he was biased about her for she knew if only she could return his feelings for her she could become the Bishop's wife. She wondered why the men who had so far gazed on her with approval were not the men she could spend a whole lifetime with. She had almost, not quite, given up hoping to meet such a man.

Miss Tremlett superintended the sports (it was half-day closing for the post office), the egg and spoon race, the sack race, and administered first aid, mostly to bruises and scratches fortunately, for those youngsters who really threw themselves into the races won prizes to offset their wounds, wounds borne with honour and pride.

After the children's tea, laid on long trestle tables in the sports field and served by Polly, Meg, Bessie and Mrs Simmonds, there was a short interval. The little ones who were too young to stay went home, while the

51

other children prepared for the exciting part of the day: the maypole, and the play.

Amelia had devised a play which would bring in all her older children. Judy was the spoilt and naughty princess, a raving beauty, Jet was Queen of the Fairies. It was a simple tale wherein the raving beauty was tamed and turned into a more beautiful and saintly creature beloved by all including, of course, the successful Prince from afar. So the play had music, fairies, princes, a queen and king, and it was a real spectacular.

Absalom was much amused by some of the actors and actresses and their amateur mistakes, but as he looked across at Amelia, engrossed, concerned, and so proud of her children, he forced himself to contain his laughter.

When the day finished and, tired and weary, the performers and organisers wended their way home, Amelia said to Absalom, 'I think Jet is more beautiful than Judy, a little thoughtful perhaps. Some people think she is shy or sad, but they misjudge her; she is neither, just steadfast.'

'It all depends who is judging beauty, Amelia.' Absalom thought for a moment, wondering whether to say what he was thinking, and then risked it. 'Judy appeals to a man because her beauty is rich and tempting. Yes, she is the eternal temptress; a man could drown all his sorrows in her arms. Jet is more the type to make a man restrain his carnal longings; she has the face of a nun.'

'Absalom!' Amelia looked shocked. 'Please remember we are talking about my schoolchildren, not ladies of a man's imagination and surely not those in the imagination of an ordained man!'

When Jet won a scholarship to the Dymchester High School for Girls Polly wasn't quite so worried about the extra expense. For one thing Meg, Judy and the twins were all at work, as she was herself. Jet's scholarship also carried a grant for non-paying pupils of the school, if this were needed, and her clothes would be easier and not so expensive as Thomas's.

At Miss Wash's Emporium Judy was Emmeline's star pupil and assistant. She was the cleverest of Polly's children in that she knew how to handle people, people she wanted to handle, of course. It worried Polly sometimes, this manipulating of people, although she wouldn't have thought of it that way. She said to Mrs P, 'I don't know how she can be like honey and not let people know how she really feels. I couldn't smile and make a fuss of someone I didn't like.'

'Oh, that's Judy practising her actressy parts. Stony says she's a real female to show 'em all what's what. He thinks she'll make the whole village sit up one day.' Mrs P thought for a moment and then said, 'Our Stony's usually right, you know Polly, and it's no good you worrying. You'll never alter Miss Judy; she knew what she could have and what she wanted as soon as she first looked in the mirror.'

Polly agreed. 'Well I'm glad Jet's not like that. She's straight as a die. She wouldn't laugh with anyone she didn't like.'

'No she wouldn't, Poll, but if anyone's going to get hurt when they goes out into the world it'll be Jet; she feels things so deep.'

Polly sighed. 'Who'd have children, Mrs P?'

'I would,' thought Mrs P but she didn't say it. She knew Polly didn't mean it and, after all, Polly's children were hers also, in a way. She'd been a lucky woman.

Jet's new school was just a few minutes away from

Thomas's Academy and they travelled to and from home together. Like Thomas, she was an ideal pupil, but unlike Thomas she was a bit of a loner. He was always popular, always a leader. Jet was proud of her brother but was surprised, when he sometimes came to meet her at her school if she were staying late, at the behaviour of her schoolfellows.

They seemed to go all coy when Thomas appeared. They weren't at all natural in front of him, and it annoyed Jet. Thomas laughed and said Jet was too serious. She must realise that other students played as well as worked. Indeed 'All work and no play' could be soul destroying.

'I'm not unhappy, Thomas, I never have been. I love my school, I love our house, I love my family. I *am* happy. Why will people assume because I don't go around giggling or blushing when a schoolboy appears, that I am a misery? Can you tell me why I should not speak to you in the same manner as I do Judy or Meg or the boys? Why do you expect me to blush or avert my eyes when I talk to you?'

Thomas laughed again and gave Jet a hug. 'My dear Jet, but I don't expect a blushing shyness from you, for I am your brother.' It was no use. Thomas wondered if his Jet would ever lower her eyes in 'maidenly modesty' when she spoke to a young man she thought attractive. 'No, she'll always face people and the world with those large, frank, open grey eyes of hers.'

But Jet was popular with the girls for although she was studious she was also helpful and patient when assistance was needed. Serious though she appeared to be, she was not a prig or a tell-tale. She received confidences from different girls for they knew their schoolgirl secrets would be safe with Bridget Bright.

The head of Dymchurch High School for Girls was

54

Dr Majorie Reynolds who was surprised by Jet's scholarship. She'd never had a village girl before, never heard of a small village school ever educating pupils to such a high standard.

Jet of course spoke about Miss Amelia Fox and what she had done for the village school at Great Little Tisbury and Dr Reynolds sent a message through Jet asking Miss Fox if she could come and see the High School. Amelia was honoured and excited. Dr Reynolds! Amelia's dream had been one day to be Dr Amelia Fox, doctor of philosophy or whatever. This Marjorie Reynolds had done it, years before Amelia was old enough even to think for herself. She was one of the pioneers, for Amelia had to admit things were getting just a bit more acceptable for women these days. Women themselves were stirring.

The visit was an absolute success, and it was the beginning of a warm friendship between the two ladies. Dr Reynolds thought Amelia a pioneer in the field of education also and was thrilled that in her god-daughter they had another dedicated soul. She, they were sure, would go to Somerville.

Amelia was driven to Dymchester in the Foxes new motor car by the new chauffeur Mr Simmonds, Eric's father, Saul having fallen by the wayside, almost literally, and transferred his services to the master at the Hall.

Perhaps some of Saul's failure was due to Boxer Plumb's deviousness and jealousy. When he heard that the Foxes were buying a car and getting Mr Albert Hilton to teach the young Saul to drive, Boxer was green with envy. He could also see Saul becoming his superior instead of his junior and learning from him.

Albert Hilton reported one day that Saul was now

capable of driving the Reverend and his sister safely and efficiently, and the evening before Saul's first drive with his employers the crafty Boxer plied the young man with home-made wine not in the best condition. Saul was a simple soul and Boxer also related the most terrible incidents which had occurred to drivers and occupants of the new-fangled machines.

Having spent a sleepless night with an upset stomach, and sent off for his chauffeur's debut by an extremely nervous mother, Saul arrived for his ordeal with a migraine. The Reverend Absalom was nervous, he hadn't wanted a car, loved the pony and trap, and his orders to Saul to drive carefully and to remember what he had been taught by Mr Hilton did not help the young man.

The car started with some loud bangs and a lot of smoke, the rector exclaiming loudly several times. All proceeded well, however, until they reached the large oak tree where two lanes crossed and where it was difficult to see what was coming.

Old Dr Skelton had been sitting under the tree while his horse was munching the grass. He couldn't be seen by Saul and of course the young man heard no horses' hooves coming down the lane. He drove on without slowing down just as the old doctor had climbed on his horse and trotted it into the lane right in the path of the car. The horse screamed and galloped off with the old doctor aboard. Saul slewed the car round and it sped for the oak tree.

He did well for he managed to stop the car a foot away, but the shouts of his passengers, the runaway horse and his own dreadful headache (he could only see half of the road his head was so painful) were too much for the young man. He alighted from the driver's seat and, holding his head, ran for home.

It was at this juncture that Jacob Simmonds appeared on the scene. He had been to the village and was on the way home. He approached the car and with great respect suggested he be allowed to drive the passengers home.

Both brother and sister were ready to shout 'No' but there was something so calm, efficient, and authoritative about Eric Simmonds's father that the Foxes resigned themselves to his mercies.

He drove the car safely back to the Rectory and Amelia asked him to wait in the study. When she and her brother had refreshed themselves and changed their dusty garments, they went into the study. In Amelia's mind a plan was forming. She still wanted to move with the times and keep the car; they weren't hurt, but perhaps Saul was too young, whereas Jacob Simmonds would be so safe with the machine. They took him into the sitting-room and asked him some questions about himself.

Neither Absalom nor Amelia had guessed the sad tale which was unfolded that afternoon; and once again Amelia was shocked to the core at the treatment meted out to the lower classes by people like herself. Yet Jacob Simmonds told his story without emotion, not seeking pity, and almost as though by his own transgressions he was responsible for his present status in life.

Jacob Simmonds had been an asylum boy, left on the steps of the workhouse one dark winter's night. His childhood was one of hardship and work in this grim institution, until, at the age of 13 he was placed in a 'good' position, that of boots boy to old Squire Blanchard, a cold and ruthless taskmaster. As so often happens when the head of a household is harsh, such an attitude spreads through the entire staff.

Jacob had learnt from an early age that meek submissiveness was the easiest way out. He was hard working and observant. Over the years in which he had 'belonged' to his master, he had progressed from lower to upper servant, boots boy to coachman. On the death of the old squire he had become chauffeur to the new squire, old Blanchard's son, Peregrine, a real chip off the old block, a heavy drinker, a womaniser, a bully of the first order.

In a strange way, however, the young squire had come to depend on Jacob. He was, on the face of it, the perfect servant, an intelligent man; not only had he mastered the rudiments of driving, he also understood an engine. Worth his weight in gold, he received the merest pittance. Of course his uniform was provided, also board and bed, and for the necessities of life his pittance sufficed.

He had very little time off from work but he was as happy as he had ever been with his circumstances: the motor car and its innards to look after, and his love for the little kitchen maid, Emily Maychem, the joy of his life, even though they lived as nun and monk in the same house. Servants needed a master's permission to marry. With the squire's uncertain temper, this could mean instant dismissal for Jacob and Emily. Without a home, without money – for little Emily too was an orphan – and perhaps with their characters blackened by the squire, where could they go? Their few precious moments together were in the kitchen, if Jacob was able to get there when the butler was away and the cook drowsy with tipple. He ate with the higher order of servants, Emily with the lower. Her life was grim, at the beck and call of the other servants, blackleading the enormous stoves, cleaning the kitchen, peeling the potatoes, she'd never even seen the squire's part of the house and would have been too terrified to ascend the stairs had she been commanded to do so. Other servants, sent upstairs for cleaning jobs, had to hide in special places in the long passages if a member of the family, or guests approached. But Jacob and Emily lived in hope, one day, one day . . .

And then it happened. The squire acquired a hunting lodge and estate some 30 miles away. He was to stay there with his party for the season. Jacob would of course be going, and he couldn't believe his good luck when Emily was ordered to accompany some other servants. He was happy too that the butler and the head cook were staying behind with the mistress. The under-cook was a little less harsh and, without the butler, there was almost a festive atmosphere among the servants.

With great secrecy Jacob made plans. He went to the tiny church six miles from the lodge. Fates were kind to the lovers for the vicar was an absent-minded old man, not interested in where Jacob came from. After three weeks of tense waiting (had he known it, at that stage there was no fear of discovery for the only people to hear the banns read were the old verger and his wife) the lovers' chance came one cold November morning; the squire had gone off early with his party for a day's shooting. The car would not be needed. The under-cook gave Emily the afternoon off and they were married in the little church with the verger and his wife as witnesses.

Their honeymoon was the brief hour they spent in the woods on the way back to the lodge. Two people had never been so happy. For the first time in their hard and lonely lives they belonged to someone. They thought no further. Something would happen, things must get better.

Six weeks later Emily knew she was pregnant. Jacob knew he must tell his empoyer they were married for Emily would be thrown out in her condition without a husband. Unfortunately the squire had been drinking heavily. Jacob asked permission for Emily to live with him in the coach house, where he had rooms; she would work until the last possible moment, and would of course work after the child was born.

'How dare you,' the squire slashed Jacob across the face with his whip. 'Fetch the strumpet to me.'

Jacob, now fearful for Emily, dashed to the kitchen, dragged Emily from the stove and ran with her from the house. When they reached the safety of the woods he told her what had happened. Jacob knew they had really done nothing wrong, except to marry without permission, but he knew the situation was hopeless; the squire could trump up any charge against him. In any case who else would employ him in that county? No one would cross the squire. The gentry were all powerful.

They walked until they were tired and hungry and slept beneath some leaves in the wood. Jacob gave Emily his coat. He thought of the little money he had saved; it was back at the coach house. Impossible to get. He had a shilling in his pocket and the next morning he went to an inn and bought bread and cheese which they washed down with water from a brook. He still had the large sum of eightpence left. They could manage for three days more, but what then? However it snowed heavily that night, and Emily was cold and exhausted. In desperation Jacob knocked at the door of a cottage, one of a pair in an isolated spot. They were the cottages of the night-soil men of Great Little Tisbury, hovels really. But the old couple took the lovers in. Sanctuary for Emily and

60

Jacob. The second night-soil man had died the day before, and a week later Jacob took his place.

On the face of it their lives were grim, and there was the tragedy of the malformed babe, Eric, but they lived in a world of their own which was probably why Jacob had remained in his job for so many years, away from a world where neither had known kindness or even fair treatment. He had transformed the two-roomed hovel into a liveable cottage. They kept a goat, a cow, chickens and pigs and their vegetable garden flourished. They had been happy in their deep love for one another; they had a togetherness few people experience.

Amelia wanted to make up for the sins of others, if not her own. Young Saul was a strong lad, a good gardener; she and her brother would see he obtained a job in the neighbourhood, Jacob would become their chauffeur and odd-job man; Boxer was getting on. And Mrs Simmonds would come as cook. Amelia wanted Meg and Bessie, as they were so young, to have the weekends off with their families. Mrs Simmonds would have the assistance of these two willing young girls during the week so no one would be overworked and all would have time off.

The upper floor of the old coach house was renovated and a delighted Jacob and his wife moved in. Jacob was always diplomatic – he'd had years of training – and Emily mothered Boxer in little ways – she'd knit him a 'westkit' for Sundays. Life for everyone at the Rectory proceeded on an even keel. The two girls teased Boxer and he enjoyed retaliating. 'They buxom lasses' were a constant source of delight to old Boxer. It was a happy household.

· However his runaway ride proved too much for the old doctor and, after church on Sunday, he informed

Absalom he had sold his practice to a younger man, James Harvey, a widower with one daughter, Angela. Miss Harvey had just left college and was to keep house for her father.

Giving the Harveys time to settle in, eventually Amelia invited them to the Rectory for dinner one evening. Half way through the meal the doctor was called away. He went quite willingly, whereas Dr Skelton would have finished his meal. James Harvey insisted his daughter stay and finish dinner. 'I am sure the rector will see you arrive home safely, my dear.'

Amelia thought about the doctor while Absalom was escorting Miss Harvey to her house. She wondered about his age. Angela had said she hadn't known her mother; she had died in childbirth. She obviously adored her father. So if Angela was about 20, then James Harvey could be 40 or over. Amelia got up and looked at herself in the mirror – not an occupation of hers. Normally a quick glance to see her hat was straight or her hair was tidy, that was all.

'I don't look much over thirty, I'm sure.' Then she reprimanded herself and wondered why she had looked in the mirror and thought about ages.

When Absalom returned he remarked that Miss Angela Harvey was a charming and most caring girl for her age.

'What's age got to do with it?' Amelia appeared irritable.

Absalom stopped what he was about to say. He looked at his sister; she looked tired. Of course she had given up so much – for him and the children – things she'd dreamed about for years.

'Amelia dear, now that you have my household running on oiled wheels, let me get a replacement for the school, and let us free you so that at long last you

62

may think of yourself and what you want for your future. You deserve that and more.'

He was surprised at Amelia's cross-toned reply. 'Don't talk so glibly, Absalom. Get a replacement just like that? I'm only here because of the replacement you *did* get. In any case, I can't leave just now. There is so much more I want to do, and I would like to see my first pupils off to university. Of course if you have other ideas as to the schoolmistress the village would like, then I should be the last person to outstay my welcome.'

Absalom had been feeling happy; Angela Harvey had been a most exhilarating companion on their walk to her home, an interesting, lovely young lady. Somehow on the way back to the Rectory his thoughts had turned to Amelia. She had always possessed an elfin beauty. He didn't want her to grow old without spreading her wings; he'd been selfish towards her all his life. Not that she is old now but . . . He was surprised and dismayed at Amelia's reaction to his suggestion.

'Oh my dear sister, oh dear, oh dear, I don't want you to go, never, never, but you do so much for us all I just thought it about time we should at least try and stand on our own two feet.'

'Your grammar leaves much to be desired, dear brother.' Whereupon Amelia burst into tears.

Absalom put his arms round her. 'There, there, Amelia, tell me what the trouble is.'

Amelia pushed her brother's arms away. 'There is no trouble at all, no trouble whatsoever, everything is absolutely fine.' The tears were still rolling down her cheeks.

'Oh I am relieved,' sighed Absalom. 'I wonder why I made such a mistake?' He passed Amelia a clean handkerchief and they both began to laugh. 'Will I ever understand the feminine gender?'

Amelia pondered her brother's question. 'Do you really want to, my dear? Although I think I understand you, I just know I do not understand myself at times.' She really was puzzled at why she did such a stupid thing as crying. She wasn't a tearful type; in any case there was nothing to cry for at that moment. 'Oh dear, perhaps I need a holiday,' she thought. 'I wonder if Marjorie Reynolds is going away with anyone? It would be good for Absalom and I to have a break from holidays together this year.'

Holidays at Great Little Tisbury were for the gentry and others whose life appeared to be one long holiday. The school was closed in the summer because there would have been no pupils at the time of year when even the smallest child could earn a few pence. The time of the fruits of the earth.

The Brights had been fortunate for summer and early autumn jobs. They lived near the Hall, a vast, rich estate. Their uncle was gamekeeper there. Mrs P had been cook there for years and still had good friends below stairs. Holidays for the gentry – hunting, shooting and fishing – always made employment for the women and children.

The Brights enjoyed it all; beating at the time of shooting, fruit picking, potato picking and of course what seemed to them the most important activity of all, gleaning. Now they were, with the exception of Jet, all at work. Polly needed the money the holiday jobs would bring. She thought she and Jet very fortunate to have influence to obtain work at the Hall and on the estate.

Jet knew she could not face beating. She felt like a murderess. She couldn't tell her mother. How could she explain something which would horrify her family and all the other country folk? 'But it's what the gentry do; it's what they always has done.' Jet could hear her mother's surprised voice.

Nobody knew about Jet's cowardice except Thomas. It was the last year he went as a beater and the first year Jet took part. She had never liked the noise of the guns, but as Polly said 'Little 'uns does get scared but they grows out of it.' It wasn't the flapping birds; she was not afraid – she was with Thomas – and she thought the birds so beautiful with their coloured plumage she wanted to paint them.

But she'd lagged a little behind and Thomas came back for her. They had to fall to the ground and roll to the edge of the covey for the guns were approaching. If the gamekeeper had seen them Thomas would have been in dire trouble and there would have been no more beating for perhaps the whole family and trouble for the gamekeeper, their uncle.

Thomas and Jet lay quietly in the rough grass. When it was safe to get up Thomas was scared at Jet's white face.

'It's all right now Jet, we can take a short cut through the copse and join up with the others. The guns have to be re-loaded and they'll wait a minute or two after the first shots. If we hurry we'll get there before the beaters' whistle goes for the next beat.'

'Let me stay here, please Thomas, no one will miss me.' Thomas decided perhaps that was the best course and he sped on his way. Jet was violently sick and really in no state to move on. She hadn't been frightened by the guns; it was worse than that.

As Thomas had dragged his sister to safety she had seen it – the beautiful bird with the lovely plumage, not strutting proudly now but lying on the ground, it's eyes closed, a bloody red spot growing black on its breast.

Later she'd heard the dogs and seen the fruits of the kill carried away. It was something she would remember all her life and ponder on how a killing can produce fruit.

This summer Thomas was going abroad as a tutor to one of the juniors at the Academy. He was ready for Oxford but had permission to tutor for a few years. He needed the money for university and he had no bother in obtaining this type of work. He was going to Italy, and Jet would miss him. She spoke to Thomas about the incident of the beating.

'It was the summer I learned that what is called sport is cruel behaviour, Thomas. I shan't help at the shoot. I'll take less money and help with the crops.'

'I know exactly what you feel, Jet, but there is no way we can even speak about it to anyone. It is the way of life here and all over England, and in the nature of things there will be changes, but now is the wrong time for both you and me. We will worry Mam and be looked upon as a little bit funny in the head. It is a time of extra work for people who are desperate for so little, Jet. Would you want to spoil it for them too? Everyone would be against your opinion of what to them is a rich sport.'

'Sport! . . . How can you call it sport? Many large grown men firing off guns at a little defenceless bird, a creature that means them no harm and would bring only beauty to this world. And how can it be sport for a mass of slobbering hounds to chase an animal? I know the fox is a killer but it doesn't need to be hunted to a state of exhaustion.'

'Of course you are right, Jet, but you must be diplomatic. People need the gentry and their occupations, and don't forget our Judy goes to the hunt now, courtesy of the influence of Grandmother Judith. Don't tell Judy that when she was bloodied on her first successful hunt you felt sick. She'll accuse you of being a coward, treat you with contempt, and it will all upset Mam, and we don't want that do we Jet?'

Of course to upset her mother was the last thing she wanted. She knew Thomas was being sensible but she did think he ought to be a bit like a young St George with the dragon.

'Oh Jet, I think the dragon in our lives is more of a monster than the one St George mastered. But don't start fighting any dragons yet. The time is unpropitious.'

'What lovely words you use Thomas.'

Thomas laughed 'Do I Jet? I hadn't noticed.'

Jet missed Thomas terribly when he went with the rich family to Italy as tutor to their son. Thomas said he would keep a daily diary and describe all the places they visited and tell her all about the people. 'And in no time we'll be together again.'

Jet couldn't imagine the weeks without Thomas but he said he would be back and, knowing he would be, she was able to get through this first lonely holiday with Thomas away and the rest in permanent employment.

Polly was worried when Jet opted for helping the seamstress at the Hall. 'Fancy sitting indoors on these lovely sunny days stitching sheets and bolster cases when you could be out with the shooting or the fruit picking.' Jet didn't mind the fruit or vegetable picking but the shooting came into the same group of activities, and Jet could not face it. She hated the look on the face of the hunter or the gunner. To her it was cruel and even bestial.

She was surprised at the people she loved who would follow the hunt or the shoot; the rector, Miss Amelia, but she wondered if, like Thomas, they were being diplomatic, believing the time not right for protest.

67

She supposed fishing was just as cruel and in the end decided to take Thomas's advice and say nothing; it would only hurt her most of all.

Polly sighed about Jet, this love child, this daughter who was to be for her, the one child always close to her mother in every way. She didn't understand Jet any more than she'd understood Thomas. Perhaps children were not meant to be close friends with their parents, but just their offspring.

'I expect it's because I had a different girlhood from lots,' she thought. 'I wonder if my mother looked for a pal in me? Dear Mum. I'll make a cake and get Stony to drop me down to her this afternoon.'

Jet was grateful for the good things which happened to her, never at any time taking them for granted or assuming they were her due. Though her mother always worked and though there had to be much scheming and sometimes illegal practices – like poaching by Stony and Boxer – to procure sustenance. Jet considered she had been the most fortunate of girls.

She had long discussions with Thomas and insisted that the poor should not be at the mercy of the rich. They had been lucky in that their mother's employer had been a generous lady, but since people were poor by chance or lowly birth and since no one has power to decide in what circumstances they shall be born, then the poor should not be victimised because of their class.

Thomas was pleased that Jet's thinking was developing along the right lines and he gently led her into a less rebellious attitude. He said she must never forget her duty to those less fortunate than she was but her resentment of her betters and the hardship she saw around her must be held in abeyance until she had learned all she could at school and college. Then she would be in a position to look around and decide with others who were compassionate what help she could give to the poor and needy.

Jet could see Thomas was right to advise her to keep her own counsel while she was powerless to do anything, but she felt a little guilty sometimes at school for not speaking out when the opportunity arose. In debates, when she thought she had been *cowardly*, not diplomatic as Thomas would have said, she sometimes caught a reproachful look in the eyes of Mademoiselle.

François Deuprez, French mistress at the High School had always had a soft spot for Jet. To her Jet was a typical English middle-class young lady. When Mademoiselle had learned that Bridget Bright was a scholarship girl, that she had no father, François was intrigued. She was a lively young teacher who found her colleagues rather serious. To them you were either an academic, single because of your career, or something outside the sphere of education.

She was interested in Jet for she thought the girl could be a contradiction. The looks, dignity and quiet behaviour could have been that of a nun, and then the flaming hair, the attractive figure, and notwithstanding what Mademoiselle recognised as tact or diplomacy, the strength of character in debate. Mademoiselle looked into those quiet grey eyes and wondered if they would ever show fire in passion. She had once seen Jet smile as she caught sight of a fair young man. François had been surprised when Jet introduced him as her brother. There was something quite contradictory about this young student.

To everyone's surprise, not least to her own, Jet was the star of the school's lacrosse team. The team was trained by Mademoiselle and once when there was an important match all Jet's family were there. Further thought and more mystery for Mademoiselle when she

met the Brights. She hoped that Bridget and her sister
Judith would never desire the same man for François
had an innate understanding of the male animal. She
could not see any she knew resisting the attractions of
Judith Bright if that young lady wanted to attract them.
The blue-black hair, the violet-green eyes, the
voluptuous figure, the lovely voice; a little husky, and
the female embodied therein. Judy possessed knowledge of her own potentiality. Miss Artful and Miss
Artless François named the two sisters to herself. 'But
why so different? What a strange family.' The twins,
Walter and William, typical young country lads of the
labouring class. Thomas, intellectual, almost aristocratic; Mrs Bright, Judith, Bridget all so different.
Bridget had her mother's colouring but that was all.
Judy was totally different again. What did she possess
of her mother? Ah, yes, that magnetism, something
which one is born with if one is fortunate. In this case,
however, the mother was unaware she possessed it, the
daughter only too aware.

She knew they lived in a small village some miles
away from Dymchester. When she learned that Mr
Bright had been drowned at sea before Bridget was
born she was filled with admiration of Mrs Bright. That
she could have survived in such a way was most
unusual. Mademoiselle was always especially kind to
Jet. She was sometimes a little bored by the majority of
students, daughters of the local big-wigs, tradesmen
etc., set in their own narrow world, not outgoing. She
hoped she would be present when Jet grew up, or at
least still in touch, but she did have a young beau over
the sea in France.

It was Amelia's idea that Jet's family should see her
in the lacrosse match. She arranged for their transport
without which she knew they wouldn't go. Polly sat

shyly watching. It was a different world from the one she'd known when young. She'd never even heard of the game. She assumed it was foreign. She could see her daughter was good, fleet of foot, sure of eye. Judy boasted that she would have been marvellous at the game but wasn't really sorry that she hadn't had Jet's opportunity.

'After all, it's only a game for girls.' She thought it a bit like ballet dancing, although most of the competitors were not like ballet dancers. The twins were slightly entertained, slightly bored and slightly amused; the game wasn't fast enough or rough enough for them. Meg had decided not to come; and Thomas pointed out the different rules to the onlookers for he too played lacrosse.

Amelia was the one most impressed, most carried away. If only she'd gone to a girls' school, if only she'd had a different father, she would have been in her element, one hundred per cent involved in everything.

Great Little Tisbury was going to war. The world had knocked on its doors at last. The village peasant was an important personage now. He was needed. The young men knew this. There was excitement in the air, a mass and united excitement; it wrapped fear around in a delicate cocoon. Trained from birth to obey, the villagers would do their duty willingly; they thought they were choosing the righteous path under their own volition; the men volunteered so eagerly; only the very rare knew there was really no other choice.

The recruiting sergeant arrived with his henchmen. They set up 'shop' in the village. Posters appeared at strategic angles round the village.

'He'm like a giant spider,' remarked Boxer as the men and youth of the village were drawn into his web.

71

A red spider of a man. Who could fail to be his happy and eager meal? A fine figure of a man in his dress uniform, curly buzby, boots like twin mirrors, waxed moustache, well fed. 'Oh what a lovely life'.

'Just wait till they lad's gits their puttees all twisted and muddy,' thought Boxer, but this was one time he didn't voice his cynical scepticism; he knew when to be silent. The voice of patriotism was too strong o'er the land.

And on a bright sunny morning the men of Great Little Tisbury marched away. It would have been jolly for the villagers to have seen their young men, husbands, and sons, embark on a train to their camp. The little train, however, plied only between the village and the nearest town, Dymchester. There was always the rumour that a loop line was going to be built, but it was still only a rumour.

Escorted by the band of the boy scouts (a few lusty buglers) they were to march to a spot eight miles from the village, past the Brights' house, where army vehicles would pick them up and take them to a place called Shotley, where they would be transformed into soldiers.

On Thomas's last night at home Jet wanted to sit with him all the time and was miserable when Polly sent her to bed as she wanted to talk to Thomas herself. But Thomas promised to come and say good-night, and Jet never forgave herself for falling to sleep before Thomas arrived, on this night of all nights.

Jet waited at the edge of the clearing, with her family, Stony and Mrs P the next morning. In the distance they heard the uneven sound of the 'band'. Her heart beat fast, she was so keyed up her legs trembled.

'They be a'comin,' yelled Stony.

And they came, a motley crew, not uniformed as yet. Caps, paper parcels under their arms. Trying to keep in step with the music. Led by a corporal in khaki, left-right, left-right. The sergeant had departed some time before for other hamlets and towns. Thomas, bringing up the rear, broke ranks as they approached the Dower House. He waved to his family and kissed Jet and his mother. Then the little band of warriors to be marched on, some concentrating on keeping in step, which appeared to pose some difficulty.

The Brights and the Plumbs went into the house. Jet stayed alone and watched the little band down the lane. They got smaller and smaller. As each row turned round the bend in the lane, the disappearance was sudden. Then Thomas took two steps back from his row, and cap in hand he waved to Jet, then he too was sucked into the void. Jet felt a long way away, and she was suddenly and violently sick.

She went into the house. Polly looked at her daughter's ashen face.

'You'll 'ave to pull yerself together, me gel. There'll be a lot for us left at home to do. Thomas wouldn't be very proud of you if he saw you now.'

Jet went upstairs and lay down on Thomas's bed. She looked round the room at his books. She would keep the attics clean and fresh while he was away and she would write him every day. It would be a journal. Lots of mothers and sisters in the village could only write short letters. She would tell Thomas about everyone at home and if he met any of the village boys while he was fighting he would have plenty to talk about.

Jet would have been very surprised to know that 'News from Home to a Soldier serving at the Front', would one day become a famous publication, designated by the experts as a 'perfect historical

73

document and a true picture of rural England during the years 1914-1918'. A cold description really for words written with love about loved ones.

Certainly Thomas and the soldiers under his command were thrilled and delighted with Jet's regular epistles, always a red-letter day, yet they arrived in the midst of mud and pain. Jet had the gift of 'nearness' in her writing; it was as though she was talking to each soldier, and he alone.

'I don't know what she finds to write about,' said Judy. Her letters were short, as though she was performing a duty. She thought her sister silly and sentimental.

A few months after Thomas had disappeared around the bend in the road Polly said, 'Well I'm glad for my mother's sake that my brothers won't be fighting, and there's Uncle Hugh; he'll be safe in Canada.' Daniel the ex-sailor/carpenter, was on ship-repair and maintenance at a dockyard, Chatham in Kent. Albert, the village grocer, was at an Army Depot in Hampshire in charge of provisions; and Joseph the gamekeeper, was still at home. 'Important war work' he said to sceptical villagers. Some of the game reserve at the Hall was now ploughed up for agriculture and Joseph was in charge of the workers, their food, hostelry etc.

So Jet was surprised to find her mother distressed at a letter from Uncle Hugh. He was on his way to the capital, either to enlist with the Canadian Forces Overseas or to set sail for home to join the British Forces. His one regret at joining up was in regard to money. His army allotment must naturally be for his wife Kathleen, so that he would have none to spare if Polly should need it (Polly always mentioned casually any *news* from Uncle Hugh; no one else ever saw the letters).

'Well he was always so good and helpful with the children when I needed a friend,' Polly always said defensively when she thought Jet was puzzled at her great pleasure in letters from Uncle Hugh. Now, in an unguarded moment, at the thought of Hugh being killed in battle, Polly had let her distress appear obvious. The money didn't matter, Jet was growing up, she'd scrape a living somehow, they'd manage, if they ever had a future together. Polly was sad in a cross way, for she was not one of those women who gloried that their loved ones volunteered for war; she would never have sneered at those men who didn't enlist as soon as they could.

It seemed to Polly that, for the family of a poor man, being a soldier made the family poorer still, for those on the home front made a better living in war time and were safe. The family of a soldier killed in action would have everlastingly to scrape for a living. True, their sons and husbands were heroes, but how long would that last?

Polly couldn't tell Hugh all this, or anyone else really. It was only her friends and a few other villagers who understood. No one voiced these opinions in public. To do so would be like having the voice of a traitor. So Polly wrote pleasantly to Hugh, as always, perhaps a little more sadly. She knew he would always do what he thought was right.

His next letter told her that he was working in Ottawa and he sent her an address. He wrote as though he was a visitor to the country, describing the lovely scenery, the wild life, the people, the city. His letters bore the censor's stamp, but Polly was content; whatever job he was doing he had given up ideas of joining up, it appeared.

She was disappointed at not seeing him again. She

75

thought she might when he wrote that he'd been told his dear Kathleen was ill through pneumonia. He thought he might take passage home to be with her. Then later he wrote that he had been advised not to come, she wouldn't have known him. His father-in-law had written that Kathleen was at last released from her suffering and mercifully her last days had been tranquil. It was ironic that, after all his years of waiting to be free to wed his loving Polly, he should be hundreds of miles away and unable to get home.

When Polly was worried about her family and the war she thought of Hugh in that distant land. He was a fine attractive man, there were many women younger, more attractive than she was, women educated to Hugh's standard, she wouldn't blame him if he met his future bride in Canada. She still wrote cheerfully and included messages from Amelia and other friends, and she was delighted when Jet began to write to her Uncle Hugh.

At the beginning of the war, and later when the first wounded began to arrive home again, Jet felt a little aloof from the mainstream of those stalwarts keeping the home fires burning.

She had been so content with her life before this terrible war had commenced. She had never wanted it to change in any way and now she was trying to come to terms with the hard fact that things would never ever be the same again. She could never let herself imagine, for one second, that she would never see Thomas again; that would have been the end. At night in the quiet house she had to will herself not to think of her last glimpse of him, his cap raised in farewell. Yet always as she closed her eyes in sleep there was the figure in relief against a red sky, its hand upraised.

In 1915 the big house, as were so many of its kind, was converted into a hospital for the wounded and a convalescent home. Polly went up there to cook, Mrs P to help generally. They kept Stony and Jet enthralled with the life at the hospital, the titled ladies, elegant and well groomed, who thought nothing of turning up their sleeves and doing a menial job, when necessary. Ladies used to being waited on now waiting on the sick and dying.

'Turrible sights, some,' said Polly, in tears. 'They call for their mothers, the young ones, just young boys'.

Judy went up to the hospital at week-ends to entertain the patients, accompanied by Mr Drake, a fine singer himself who had never dreamed that in the boredom of retirement from Covent Garden he would be presented with such a promising pupil. Alma Drake started a dramatic society. Judy's feet had been firmly placed on the ladder of opportunity. True, she worked tirelessly to learn the craft of acting and never missed the breathing exercises and boring part of her singing lessons, but opportunity had come through the war and she had to hide her feelings of elation at the wonderful world in front of her.

'Judith takes everything in her stride,' said a proud Mizwash.

Not too much, however was expected of Jet. For one thing she was in her last years at the High School and Miss Reynolds's eagle eye was on this star pupil of hers.

Bridget Bright was the spearhead of Dr Marjorie Reynolds's attack to realise her dream for the future of English womanhood. Marjorie, daughter of a Yorkshire farmer, had fought her way to the top in education. She would ensure that girls of Jet's class, who formerly had no chance in the field of education or indeed life, would have the opportunities denied to

77

their mothers.

She knew that Jet would be expected to do something for the war effort – she now had three brothers in France for Wheel and Wally had joined Thomas – but Miss Reynolds thought that the writing Jet did daily in her war diary, plus the extra housework and cooking she was doing so that her sister and her mother could work full time for the soldiers at the Hall, was more than enough. She thought Bridget's sister Judith could have helped with the housework at their home but Jet insisted Judy's time was better spent entertaining the men for 'she brings great comfort to them and makes them forget, even for a little while, their pain and suffering.'

That Jet liked housework would have surprised and perhaps disappointed Miss Reynolds who wanted girls of Jet's intellect for the 'pioneer' corps of her dreams. Jet thought the Dower House looked so beautiful with the care lavished on it, on the tiled kitchen floor, the shining wooden floors and bannisters, the leaded light windows, the heavy oaken front door. She sensed the love that this house exuded because it had been loved. Polly always said, 'Oh it's a lovely house,' and the rest of the family agreed, but they wouldn't be sad about living any where else. Thomas and Jet would leave half themselves behind were they ever forced away.

Amelia held a 'Comforts for the Troops' class regularly at the Rectory. Jet knitted Thomas a long scarf, mittens and socks, hoping that he would be home before he needed more, but, with other ladies of the village, she lost count of the total number of garments they knitted. So expert had they become that they hardly glanced at their work.

Angela Harvey was a VAD in France and her father had taken over for a younger doctor who had joined up, so he journeyed to more villages and was very busy. Angela knew her father was over-conscientious and Amelia had promised to keep an eye on him.

Absalom, that man of peace, had gone to war. It had been a shattering experience for him. The suffering of the soldiers, their obedience to command, the strength of character of the ordinary man, all served to strip him of the veneer he formerly possessed, or thought he possessed. He refused to take leave; his first duty was to the soldiers. At one time Amelia was quite concerned for he seemed so embittered. She said to James Harvey, 'He makes me feel guilty because I'm a civilian. It is as though he has only thoughts and feelings for the men at war, and we civilians are not worthy of them.' One of the brighter spots in his war-torn life had been the chance meeting with Angela Harvey while visiting some wounded at her hospital.

The temporary incumbent at the Rectory was the Reverend Ezekial Tozer, a tall, thin, sallow, sepulchral looking man of 55, a holy man who lived by the articles of the Church, not for the love of his flock. He wished he had been born a century before. He acted as though he had. He even wore the old-fashioned flat hat of the country parson of the past. It was tethered by a black cord to the top of his cassock.

Amelia disliked the Reverend Ezekial on sight. He took possession and charge of the Rectory and then told her she must look upon his stay as purely temporary. She must look upon the Rectory as her home and must stay until the Lord in his infinite mercy saw fit to bring her dear brother home again.

The new temporary vicar possessed a plaintive invalid wife (shades of my mother, thought Amelia!) and Amelia could see herself becoming a superior servant in the household (if not a handmaiden, she

79

thought) and she couldn't wait to get away. She bought the little white cottage next to the school, taking great joy in removing from under Ezekial's jealous gaze, all Absalom's books and pictures from the study.

'Such a pity to disturb them,' remarked the Reverend.

Amelia's cottage had originally been two cottages so the rooms were of a good size. Everyone joined in and helped with the decorating. The floors were of solid oak and Jacob and Stony Plumb waxed and polished them. Mizwash and Judy made the curtains and cushions and Boxer enjoyed superintending the laying out of the garden. The doctor presented Amelia with two beautiful Chinese rugs. He'd bought them before the war and had not bothered to unpack them; he was never long enough at home to enjoy his house. There was a bed-sitting-room for Emily Simmonds. Jacob had gone to London to be chauffeur/batman to his son, Eric who had become a person of some importance at the War Office. He had been responsible for an invention connected with anti-Zeppelin warfare.

Eric was coming down to the village for a weekend's respite and Amelia decided that it would be a good idea to have a house-warming then, in spite of the war and austerity. It would also be a 'thank-you' for all the kind friends who had helped her.

Eric, who was staying at the Bull Hotel, would be coming to dinner, and so Polly and Mrs P took charge of the kitchen, for Amelia insisted that Emily and Jacob should sit down with their son. The doctor was free that evening as his cousin Alasdair, also a doctor, had been invalided out of the army and was coming as a partner in the practice. On the spur of the moment she invited the matron of the hospital, Helen Fraser, who wondered if she could bring two young officers who were convalescing and were a little homesick. Judy was going to sing after dinner so Amelia asked Miss Wash and the Drakes. She thought she could hardly leave out Miss Tremlett and her mother.

Amelia felt a little guilty that her little 'house-warming' was turning into a party, fourteen guests, but she wouldn't say too much about it to Absalom in her letters. In any case all her guests were doing their bit on the home front.

Polly and Mrs P surpassed themselves with the meal. Consommé, Pheasant (Amelia paid Boxer for them but forbore to ask from whence they came!) soufflé, and raspberrries and cream. Jacob and Emily disappeared into the kitchen after dinner, where Polly and the Plumbs had eaten. Emily made coffee and the entire 'kitchen' staff washed the dinner things, having a festive occasion of their own.

Then Judy sang, Miss Wash accompanied her on the piano, and Jet noticed for the first time what other people had seen for a long while. Judy's hair was coiled loosely in the nape of her neck, her frock was a beautiful blue, classically simple, her eyes seemed deep violet in the glow of the lamps, her skin white, against the blue-black hair. Her voice had the pure tone of a choirboy, yet it had a magnetic quality a boy's would lack. The room was hushed, the audience spellbound. Judy finished her recital with a lullaby. Amelia wiped her eyes. James squeezed her hand gently.

Jet felt far away, an observer, an unseen watcher. The two young officers went over to talk to Judy. She appeared calm and aloof. One of them wrote something on a piece of paper, folded it and handed it to her. Jet wondered idly what it was. Eric was talking to Amelia. Could that distinguished-looking man with the solemn brown eyes be the stuttering child of that

81

world before the war? One only noticed his deformed back when he stood up. She thought with love and gratitude of Amelia. Where would they all be now, if she had not come into their lives?

The doctor was laughing at something Boxer had told him. Tiggy Taylor, the local poacher, was now a sergeant in France and a private in his troop was the former gamekeeper who had waged relentless war on him! The doctor was also amused that he had been able to shock Boxer. Young Saul, was a despatch rider, at the moment in Angela's hospital in France, only slightly wounded. He had been mentioned in despatches for bravery.

Judy was playing softly on the piano, the two young men by her side. One of them said something which made her smile and he looked delighted. The Drakes and Tremletts were chatting happily with Miss Wash, Matron, Amelia and James in another little group. Everybody has somebody thought Jet, but I only want Thomas to be here. Where was he now when everyone was laughing and happy? Was he lying wounded in a muddy trench? She felt a surge of panic. She had to leave this room. She must get home. She stood up as Eric came across to her.

'How is Meg, Bridget?' he asked. Jet didn't want to talk, she had to get back to the house.

'Meg and Bessie were kind to me at school, I remember them with gratitude and affection during those lost dark days.' Jet looked at him. Suddenly ashamed of her anti-social attitude – everyone was suffering in some way or other at the present time – she said, 'Oh, the girls gave us all a shock. They volunteered for munitions work, somewhere in London at a place called Woolwich. They lodge with a Mrs Hubbard at Plumstead, a motherly soul. They are very happy. Surprising, isn't it?'

'Not at all,' Eric smiled. 'They are the strong lode which runs a straight and reliable course, keeping us erratic mortals steady. If you will let me have Meg's address I would like to visit her.'

Her mother and the Plumbs were ready to leave. Jet decided to go with them. Judy would not lack for an escort home when the party decided to break up. At the moment there was no sign of it. They walked home, arm in arm. Boxer now lived with his brother and Mrs P, having left the Rectory.

'Can't abide "Killer Tozer". He warn't arf in a paddy. What about the graves? I tell 'im I'll always come back to dig yourn reverence!'

Ezekial Tozer blamed Amelia for the 'immigration' of the Rectory servants, thinking her a most un-Christian lady for a clergyman's brother, and a mill-stone round the Reverend Fox's neck.

Amelia was waiting for James Harvey. He'd sent a note to the school, hurriedly written. 'Have momentous news for you. Will call this evening.' She had sent a reply to the surgery inviting him to dinner. Now she was waiting, impatient for this 'momentous news', imagining all sorts of amazing happenings.

Had he accepted a practice elsewhere? She felt depressed at the thought. Her life had become part of his now that they were both alone; ah, but perhaps it was only on her part, perhaps she was the one who had become dependent on the friendship of this fine man. Yes, that was it; he was going away.

She thought this the worst news he could have for her. Then she recalled the night of her house-warming and his close conversation with the matron from the hospital. She remembered the feelings of jealousy she had experienced for one moment when she had seen them laughing together. She had dismissed her feelings. 'I'm an old schoolmarm. Who'd want me?'

Yes, that was it; James was to marry the matron. A widower and widow, they had the same interests. She was a fine-looking woman, older than Amelia by about five years. That pleased Amelia a little until she dismissed her uncharitable thoughts. She thought of the matron. A charming woman, tall, fair, cool, efficient. Yes, she'd take charge of James and his practice, it would run on oiled wheels. That was what a doctor needed. James had a daughter, the matron a son; she knew they were of the same age. 'Perhaps *they*'ll marry, Angela and her John – an ideal family.'

She wished she hadn't made such an effort to look nice this evening. Well, it was too late to change now, he'd be here at any moment. Miss Wash had made her a frock from a discarded one of her mother's. It was in a burgundy velvet. It suited her dark curly hair which she kept short. It made her look young and a little boyish. On the spur of the moment she had fished out her mother's ruby necklace and little stud ear-rings. Daringly, a dusting of face powder and of all things, lipstick. She had thought for a moment, gazing into the mirror, 'Well old girl, you really could be something!' Now she felt like a painted woman.

She had never seen her mother wearing the lovely velvet gown, or necklace and ear-rings. Had she worn the dress, a young girl in love with that stern man, the Dean? Perhaps in his youth he'd been different, perhaps he had appeared just masterful to the feminine creature her mother was. For a moment she felt sad for her ineffectual mother. In the old days she'd had no daughterly feelings for the poor creature, no womanly compassion. Now, fleetingly, she wished her mother back. 'How cold and hard I was in those unhappy days.'

She had given Emily Simmonds the night off. Emily had gone to stay with Mrs Tremlett while Miss Tremlett and Miss Wash were dining with two middle-aged travellers at the Bull. Amelia smiled as she thought of the two spinsters fluttering their way through the evening. 'Well, that's me, too,' she decided. 'I'll dash upstairs, scrub my face and put on my old blue woollen frock.' She was cross with herself as she went towards the stairs, remembering how girlishly flattered she'd felt earlier in the evening at Mrs Simmond's 'Oh, Miss Ameelee, how lovely you be lookin'.' Now she felt naked. Emily Simmonds must have thought in her heart, 'There's Miss Amelia trying to catch a husband'. But Emily Simmonds had been startled at the sight of Amelia. The words were spontaneous, she hadn't meant to remark on her employer's appearance; it wasn't done. She really thought that Amelia looked radiant and, romantic like most women, she wanted the handsome doctor to be in love with her beloved mistress. They'd both done so much for the village folk.

Too late. As Amelia climbed the stairs, James rang the bell. She opened the door, trying to look calm and businesslike.

'Good evening, my dear. Oh how charming you look this evening.'

'Pssh', thought Amelia crossly, taking his hat and coat. She led him into the drawing-room.

'Let's have a sherry while you tell me this momentous news.'

'I'd love a drink,' said James, 'but as you've invited me to dinner, I shall keep you in suspense until we've eaten. I won't spoil your meal, for you won't eat when you hear my news.'

'Conceited ass,' said Amelia to herself. She was very

bad tempered now. 'So he thinks I'm fond of him and will be upset to hear he's marrying Helen Fraser.' Her mind moved quickly; suppose she got in first, after dinner, she could say she had decided to get away from Great Little Tisbury. She decided to receive his news coolly and with the usual congratulations. She already had in mind the compliments she would pay the matron.

The dining-room looked welcoming, romantic too, with the polished silver candlesticks. The meal was all ready, Mrs Simmonds had seen to that. She just had to serve it and appear the efficient hostess to a family friend, one of many.

It was a chilly evening and James obviously enjoyed the chicken casserole done in Mrs Simmonds's special way with mushrooms and vegetables. They finished with one of James's favourite sweets, caramel custard.

'Let's take our coffee into the drawing-room, then I shall be all ears, James.' An unfortunate choice of words which made her smile; yes, she was a big-eared donkey.

'Good,' said James. 'Do you know, that's the first time you've smiled all evening? Perhaps you are tired? Well I'll keep you in suspense no longer.' Amelia turned her face away from James as he at last unfolded the momentous news which had sent her frantic with worry all evening.

'Angela and Absalom are married!' Amelia closed her eyes. It *was* momentous, something she hadn't visualised in her wildest dreams, it was all the more wonderful because it wasn't the news she was expecting. 'Absalom will be writing you,' said James. Apparently they had had an afternoon off in the midst of chaos.

'Oh, it really is wonderful news, James! I hope you

are as pleased as I am; my brother is indeed a most fortunate man.'

'I couldn't be happier, Amelia, although I shall miss her terribly, but she is ecstatic and I am happy for her.'

Quietly he told her of his life with his daughter. He had married, in his youth, the sister of his college friend. They were both ridiculously young, ridiculously happy, he a struggling doctor. She had become pregnant soon after they were married and had died tragically giving birth to her daughter. Because of medical ethics he had been unable to attend his wife at the birth of their child and had tortured himself ever since wondering what would have happened had he been there. Now Amelia could see why James was so insistent on attending every village birth, even the straight-forward ones the local midwife had always managed formerly.

'And, my poor Amelia, what will you do now?'

'Poor, poor? What on earth do you mean, what will I do now?' She was quite sharp with the doctor. 'As a matter of fact, only today I had made up my mind it was time I moved on. I would like to go to college and study. Like many women, especially those with fathers such as mine, I was robbed of the chance of a real education.'

The doctor looked discomfited, suddenly weary as though the life had gone out of him.

'It was just as well I didn't. . .' He seemed to be talking to himself.

Amelia stood up, yawned, removed her ear-rings and said in the strict tones of the schoolmistress, 'Well, if you don't mind James, I am a little tired. It has been a busy day.'

He was profuse with apologies and, grabbing his hat and coat from Amelia, he was gone. She bolted the door slowly and sat on the bottom stair in the hall. She wondered why she felt so desperately miserable. Some of Absalom's happiness should have rubbed off on her; it was all she ever wished for him. 'Of course I'm happy for him.' She burst into tears just as the doorbell rang.

The letter box was lifted and two eyes peered through. 'Are you there, Amelia? I am so sorry, I left in such a hurry I forgot my bag. I came straight to you this evening, from a patient.'

'Blast,' thought Amelia. 'Where's my handkerchief? I'll have to open the door.' James came in. Amelia reached for his bag and handed it to him.

'Why you are crying? Oh my dear, aren't you well?'

'I'm perfectly well, thank you James.' She had intended to be brusque, anxious for him to leave again. Her wretched tears fell down her cheeks and in a moment she really was crying, uncontrollably.

And this is how Amelia got her man! James's arms were round her and he was murmuring all the words, the simple words which have been murmured over the centuries. By the time her tears were stemmed, she was betrothed. They sat by the fire in the drawing-room.

'I thought you were tired.' James laughed and Amelia was in his arms again. 'I'll wait only the three weeks necessary to put up the banns. Angela is coming home very shortly and she hoped to persuade Absalom to come with her on leave. Won't they be surprised?'

They would have a quiet wedding. People had no right to such happiness at such a time; yes, a quiet wedding. A honeymoon could wait until the dreadful war was over. It surely must be soon, almost four years of misery. But for once in her life Amelia was weak and allowed herself to be led by the ladies of the village. She must have a white wedding. As soon as Polly heard the news she arrived with what she called, '*the* wedding dress'. It had been Lady Margaret's in another century. It was a work of art, beautifully preserved. Parchment coloured, tiny tucks from waist to mandarin neck. So expertly cut, the gown possessed its own miniature train. Everything had been complete in the trunk in the Bright's attic. For some reason Polly had refused to let Judy unpick it for the material as they had done with most of the other fine clothes willed by Lady Margaret to Polly. The headdress and veil, the blue gown for a bridesmaid, even the gloves.

Amelia thought herself stupid, but she was as excited as a girl. They would keep it secret from the bride-groom. Jet would look sweet in the blue bridesmaid's dress. The ladies of the village took charge of the reception. In the village hall, they'd manage a buffet breakfast. There was one thing which Amelia was sure would spoil her day; Ezekial Tozer. She felt depressed when she imagined herself making her vows to him.

James knew that if Amelia could be married by Absalom her happiness would be complete, and so he kept a secret from her. Absalom was trying to come with Angela on leave, but naturally the welfare of his men came first. Anyway he would do all he could, if his officiating would make Amelia happy. James daren't tell Amelia. If Absalom didn't arrive for the wedding, it would be a bitter disappointment; better she thought Absalom was unable to come.

James took Miss Tremlett into his confidence. Eager to be part of the proceedings, she promised to sit by the telegraph machine night and day if, as now seemed possible, Absalom would be able to get to England, but at rather a late hour.

Thus it was that at 2 o'clock one dark night Ethel Tremlett could have been seen throwing stones at Dr Harvey's bedroom window. The doctor put his head out

89

of the window.

'They'll arrive in London late on Tuesday night.' The wedding was on Wednesday afternoon.

'Good, I'll tell Amelia.'

Miss Tremlett went back across the road to the Post Office, which was opposite the doctor's lovely ivy-covered Georgian house. James, now excited for Amelia, decided he'd pop across and tell her. Returning home, he didn't see the Reverend Tozer approach round the corner of the school (he was walking his dog) for he'd left a radiant Amelia. As he approached his house Miss Tremlett appeared from the shadows.

'In my excitement I forgot to tell you that Eric will bring Mr and Mrs Fox down from London with him on Wednesday morning. They will start early and will be here at about 11. They are staying at Eric's flat on Tuesday night.'

James was indeed pleased. He had been wondering on the way back from Amelia's cottage whether he had been too eager to convey the glad tidings to her, there might be a problem of trains at the last minute. He grabbed Miss Ethel Tremlett, placed a kiss on her cheek and said, 'Thank you, thank you for both of us.' She giggled hysterically as the Reverend Tozer approached. He touched his hat.

'Oh dear, he must have seen us. Oh dear, I am not respectably clothed.' She was in her nightdress, long dressing-gown and boudoir cap, James in his pyjamas and dressing-gown.

In her agitation she dashed across the road, and, unused to bedroom slippers on the rough surface, she slipped and fell. James went to her rescue, and with one arm around her he saw her home.

'Oh dear, what will the Reverend think?' Miss

90

Tremlett was quite worried.

'Well he'll think evil of me for he saw me leaving Amelia's in this same state of undress. If he was marrying us on Wednesday I should explode when he came to the "just impediment" part, or perhaps he'd then announce that he was the one who knew. But what the dickens was he doing out this time of night?'

Miss Tremlett was suddenly belligerent. 'He has communication with the Widow Starkey at the other side of the village. He walks his dog *every* night.'

James yelled with laughter, 'Well he'd better be careful, or he'll be in excommunication one day.' Miss Tremlet screamed hysterically and went into her house laughing.

Ezekial had paused in the shadows watching the end of the episode. A doctor too! He'd left the school-mistress's cottage and then gone home with Miss Tremlett. And then their behaviour in the street, and in such clothing. He was shocked. Then he remembered he was to marry James and Amelia on Wednesday. So that was it, James Harvey had obviously been 'interested' in the schoolmistress *and* the post mistress. He had chosen Amelia. Perhaps Miss Tremlett was proving difficult in retiring from the scene? Certainly the Reverend Ezekial was surprised at her brazen behaviour. He made a mental note to be observant on his nightly walks abroad.

Amelia's wedding day. The promise of a fine sunny day. It started with a lovely surprise. Jacob arrived with Eric, Angela and Absalom, before breakfast. Angela had insisted they drive through the night. Over breakfast they took note of the day's schedule. Angela went off to see her father, promising Amelia that she'd

91

snatch a few hours sleep in her old room. Absalom was packed off to bed. He had wanted to see the Reverend Tozer, to tell him he would be officiating at his sister's wedding, but Amelia said he'd never get away from the Rectory in time to rest before dressing for the wedding. Mrs Simmonds was therefore despatched with a note to the Rectory.

Jacob went off to sleep in his wife's room, Eric to the Bull. Amelia and Mrs Simmonds tidied up, prepared a light buffet lunch for noon, and Amelia went off to lay out her wedding clothes. At 1 o'clock Judy arrived with Miss Wash to superintend the dressing of the bride and bridesmaid. Judy was so clever with Jet's thick hair and the two sisters had a happy time. They chatted about the past, what they hoped for the future. Judy was sure she would be in London training to be an actress, perhaps sooner than anyone thought. Jet didn't say she wasn't aware anyone did think such a thing.

But Judy said, 'You're much nicer now you've grown up, Jet. Must you go to college and all that study? Why not come to London with me? You could be a teacher there, if you wanted.'

'I couldn't leave the house while Thomas is away.'

'Oh I forgot, it's always Thomas with you, isn't it?' Judy would have gone on further. Jet really must make an attempt to break this strange link she had always had with Thomas; she must make a determined effort to be independent. But she said no more. They'd had a happy time together, a rare event for the sisters. She'd be bound to upset Jet if she said any more, and Amelia wouldn't want a miserable bridesmaid. 'There, Jet, you're ready, and you look pretty enough to be the bride.'

Eric arrived. Amelia had asked him to give her away and he was proud and honoured by her request. Miss

Wash came downstairs with the bride and they gasped; Amelia looked so beautiful. Miss Wash was flattered; it was fortunate she had always been gifted in this matter of ladies' gowns for every occasion. (She had only assisted in the dressing of the bride!)

Polly arrived with the bouquets. 'Oh Miss Amelia, how truly lovely you are. Wouldn't it have been wicked if I'd let Judy unpick that beautiful gown?'

'I shall take great care of it, Polly, and perhaps two other brides will wear it one day.'

Miss Wash felt suddenly old. If only Amelia had said three brides. Even though they would all have smiled, it wouldn't have been so obvious. Amelia realised she had hurt Miss Wash's feelings. On this day of days she wanted everyone to be happy, to forget the war for a brief while. She bent forward and kissed Miss Wash on the cheek.

'Emmeline could make herself a gown even more lovely than this. Thank you for all you have done, my dear.' Miss Wash's spirits revived; the compliment had worked, as compliments always did with her.

And so to church. Miss Tremlett at the organ, the choirboy pumping hard. As the strains of the Wedding March filled the little church, James rose with his best man, turned and faced his bride.

He'd been kept in the dark as to what she would wear and at the sight of this ravishing creature he caught his breath for a moment and then, forgetting the procedure, he hurried down the aisle towards her, kissed her and brought her to where Absalom was standing. The wedding guests laughed and so did Amelia.

'This would never have done for Ezekial.' whispered James. Amelia laughed again. Absalom looked very serious but conducted the service beautifully.

As they left the church James asked his bride, 'Tozer wasn't there, was he?'

'I shouldn't think so,' said Amelia.

James laughed. 'I expect he's takng tea with the widow.' Amelia was puzzled. She really must remember to ask James what he meant by that remark.

The village hall was crowded; it was like a festival, and the happy couple were despatched with rose petals and an old boot on the car even though they were only driving across the road to James's house. That evening they would dine quietly with Angela and Absalom. It would be better than a honeymoon; they had so much to talk about.

Amelia was sad to learn that Absalom and Angela were going back to France. It seemed like tempting Providence to her. There was much they could do in the hospitals here amongst the wounded. She wondered if the maxim, 'It is better to have loved and lost than never to have loved at all,' was true. Before, she had been philosophical about events, but now she was fearful for her brother, away in danger again, his young wife, if not at the front, at a hospital which experienced shelling. For James, for herself. Perhaps one day she would get used to loving and being loved, yet she didn't ever want to have an attitude of 'so be it' about something which she prayed would always be as precious to her as it was now.

Jet was alone in the Dower House. She never minded being alone, and indeed in this house she never felt solitary. The house always held a welcome for her, it always had. When she was little, however tired she was, she always ran the last few steps to the door.

In any case there was so much to do these days. She had always kept Thomas's rooms and her own clean and tidy. Now that her mother was working at the hospital so much Jet cleaned the rest of the house too. This was a great help and relief to Polly, but Jet did it half as much for the house as for her mother. It was a lovely house to come into, the black-and-white tiled entrance hall, the shining mahogany bannisters on the curving stairway, flowers in the hall, flowers everywhere. In winter, autumn leaves and attractive foliage.

She had wrapped her bridesmaid's frock in tissue paper and put it back in the trunk in the attic.

'I shan't be a bridesmaid again.' Not that 'once was enough'. Meg was to marry one of the Hubbard sons in London on his next leave. It would be a quiet wedding. Polly was going 'Up Lunnon' for the first time in her life. Jet felt badly about declining to go with her mother. She couldn't leave the house while Thomas was away.

'It'll be theer when we come back, gel.' Yet her mother was very good about it. She was being unkind and unreasonable but she just could not explain the panic which overcame her at the thought of going round that bend to London. She knew she would not get back. She *must* wait at the house for Thomas's return.

The war seemed to be moving tragically nearer the Dower House when news came that Thomas had been captured. The family was sad and worried. They'd heard dreadful stories of the ill treatment of prisoners at the hands of the Germans. Nobody knew how these snippets of news got back to the folks at home but someone had a friend whose son, or husband, had become enormously and unhealthily fat because prisoners were fed on a diet of stewed horses heads and stale cabbage. Or a prisoner was a skeleton because of not being fed at all.

95

Jet got in touch with the Red Cross and made a collection for the local prisoners of war; knitted hats, scarves, gloves, etc., and what food and sweets they could spare. It appeared that only Thomas, who was an officer, and one of his men were made prisoner during a skirmish. The private was trapped away from his companions. He would have been killed had not Thomas gone back for him, rescued him but escaped into another ambush where they were captured.

Although everyone was worried about Thomas and Jet could hardly sleep at times for thinking of the prisoners in Germany, part of her rejoiced in the fact that Thomas would one day be free; for however prisoners are treated they are not killed and one day they come home. So going without small luxuries to send to the prisoner-of-war camp was no hardship. Thomas was alive! She was lucky, they were all lucky.

The war dragged on. Jet was at home when the telegram came. Polly was in the garden pegging out some clothes. A bird was singing, the sun was shining, and Polly was singing. To Polly afterwards it seemed as though when she stopped singing the sun went in and the little bird stopped his singing. Wheel had been killed on the Somme. Polly wondered vaguely where Wally was. Why wasn't his name on the telegram too? It was always Wheel *and* Wally, William and Walter Bright, never apart, never separated. They had somehow courted the same girl, Emily Newbold from the village; a threesome then but Emily didn't seem to mind, and Wheel, the victor, seemed to expect that Wally would go on their honeymoon with them.

Polly prayed that Wally had escaped in the Somme Battle. She somehow felt it would comfort Emily to know that one of the twins had survived. She thought that perhaps Emily loved both boys as both boys had loved her. If only Emily had been twins too.

Olive Tremlett brought the telegram to Polly. Emily was away from the village at the moment being midwife to her sister. Perhaps it would be better for Polly to be with Emily when she got the sad news. Olive Tremlett put her arms around Polly. They had been at school together. Polly had suffered under Miss Batty's tyranny, and Olive had always liked her, admiring her for the way she hadn't let the harsh discipline affect her, her sunny nature, her kindness to the little ones at school and her very joyousness at being alive. Olive had felt guilty for she had been treated with favour by Miss Batty; Olive's mother was that personage of importance, the Postmistress.

Polly had always liked Olive Tremlett too, grateful to her for the little ways she'd tried to help at school, sorry too that she was still unmarried, for she knew Olive liked children and would have loved to have been married.

'Her bloomin' mother's fault,' Mrs P always said.

Olive took Polly indoors and made tea. Polly had so much compared to her, money apart, but she had lost so much more. She wondered if it was better to have loved and lost than never to have loved at all. In the pain in Polly's eyes, she doubted it.

Some weeks later came the news that Wally was in hospital at Salonika and would be coming back to England at any time. Then they heard that he had been wounded in the leg, and would be invalided out. Polly bustled about getting a downstairs room ready for the wounded soldier. She wondered how he would be, not because of his gammy leg, but because, having lost Wheel, he would be only half a person.

It was at this time, 'of all times', moaned Polly, that

Judith Bright became ill. She had a daily woman but of course she was only a domestic; Mrs Bright needed to be looked after. There was no one else and Polly went to stay with her. Judy was very good: 'Well I had the sweets. I must take the sour with good grace,' she said to Polly; and every evening after work she came to help nurse the invalid who only came to life when Judy appeared, and this gave her mother a break.

Polly thought she would have hated it but somehow, perhaps because of the helplessness of the once-proud woman, she felt sorrow and compassion for her mother-in-law. 'She could have had the real love of me and mine,' thought Polly, 'and all we would have wanted in return was her love. We didn't want her money really.' She smiled when she remembered that at one stage in her life she had actually needed Mrs Bright's money, although they didn't get it. 'Well, you know what I mean.' Polly often spoke to an invisible being, her other self perhaps.

Judy cried when her grandmother died, and Polly had a lump in her throat at the end for Judith Bright had said to her, 'I wish I had the chance to make it all up to you, Polly.' Polly patted her mother-in-law's cheek and said, 'It don't matter, really it don't.' Then Judith said, 'Hold my hand Judy. Be kind to your mother, and thank you for everything.'

At the funeral Polly was glad she had looked after her at the end. They went back to the house to meet the solicitor, Judy asking her mother to accompany her for it was a foregone conclusion that the estate had been left to her.

Uncle Daniel was very concerned about Wally. There was nothing for him at the Dower House. His mother was out all day as were Judy and Jet. He'd have nothing to do, nothing to see, all day to think of his dead brother. There was also the probability that he would be in pain. Daniel, who had been released from Chatham because of deafness, was doing quite well in the carpentry line in the village, and he only had himself to think of, but there were two small rooms above his little shop; they were not suitable for living accommodation for anyone else, and anyway were always crammed with spare wood from the shop.

So when he heard of Judy's inheritance, he went to see her to ask what she intended to do with her grandmother's house. Did she want to let it or did she want to sell it? Daniel couldn't buy such a house in a lump sum but he could put some capital down and pay the rest off 'all legal like', and perhaps Wally might want to live there too. Judy didn't want to stay in Great Little Tisbury. This was her chance of getting away even though it had come sooner than she had wanted. She would grasp the opportunity. Amelia and the doctor introduced her to a solicitor who would advise her. She sold the house to her uncle and had not only some capital but also a weekly income.

Mr Drake took her to London to meet an actor-manager he knew. As a result of her interview she was to be a live-in pupil. The actor-manager's wife was also an actress, so Judy lived in the perfect environment. She did all sorts of jobs in the theatre and when reading her letters home Polly wondered at the change. 'She'd never have done all that work here,' thought Polly.

Jet thought Judy very brave. She could not have gone into a strange house, eating, washing, talking, living with people from a different background and feeling at home as Judy, a chameleon if ever there was one, did. When Judy wrote home it was as though she had lived in that St John's Wood house with those

99

theatrical people for ever, a daughter of the house, a beloved daughter, seemingly.

Polly wished Jet was as single-minded as Judy. She had passed her exams with flying colours but refused to go up to Somerville until after the war.

'I don't know what all the fuss is about,' remarked James; 'Bridget is bound to marry one day.' He was a little taken aback by Amelia's fury at his 'typical remark of an anti-feminist male'. He thought her unfair since he believed that all people should be helped to achieve whatever they wanted in the way of a career. 'Perhaps I have expressed myself badly, and for that I apologise dear, but you will never alter Bridget from her desire to stay here until the war is over. She will, in any case, become a teacher; it is what she wants. Why can't she take over from you? You'll be leaving soon. You *must* rest more.'

Amelia was expecting their first child. Perhaps this was the way out for everyone concerned. She had been anxious to hand over the school to the right woman. Who better than Jet?

Jet jumped at the chance. She'd be at home still, at the Dower House, and people would stop trying to force her into doing something she didn't want at the moment.

Dr Reynolds was furious. Jet protested that she would still keep up with serious study. Amelia had her father's extensive library – Absalom was not interested in keeping the books. The Reverend Tozer too had a wonderful collection of books. Jet was welcome there whenever she wished; she was one of the rare villagers who had been able to communicate with the taciturn and severe Ezekial. She realised he was a man without most of the emotions possessed by others and treated him accordingly, accepting him for what he was, a neutral, a cipher.

100

Jet loved teaching in the village school and she enjoyed studying in her free time. As the war dragged on she looked forward to better news from the front. She had so much to tell Thomas in her letters, and she was thrilled to hear that he was well as a prisoner of war, and that his friends were wonderful chaps, cheered that we were at last 'beating the Hun'.

Wally came home. He had naturally returned to the Dower House at first, but the memories of Wheel were too strong at the old home and, off the beaten track, it was quiet and depressing, so Emily Newbold went to live in Judith Bright's old house to be housekeeper for Wally and Daniel. Wally, who had hated visiting his grandmother's house when she was alive, now settled down so happily in it that Jet was surprised.

'Oh it's different now, Jet. Emily's no Grandmother Bright and she does Uncle Dan'l and me proud. We don't seem to have lost Wheel so much when us three is together.' And Jet found on her visits to Wally that the old house had grown warm and inviting under Emily's care.

Polly understood why Wally had left home. She visited him often and got on well with Emily who had loved both Polly's sons. She wondered what she'd do without the Plumbs and Jet. Everything seemed to be changing so, and the war was dragging on. Surely it should have been over by now?

Then great, great excitement. A visitor for the Dower House. To Jet, an old lodger of her mother's who had become a lifelong friend; to Polly, her love, the father of her last baby. Jet was surprised after her first few hours with Uncle Hugh, how relaxed she was with him, how easy he was to talk to, not in the least like a stranger; it was as though she had known him all her life. She thought perhaps it was because her mother had spoken of him and his kindness to her children; and his help in getting an education for Thomas whose intelligence he recognised.

Jet knew her Uncle Hugh had just returned from Canada where he had been working for the government, and that he was going on to take up forestry work in Scotland.

She enjoyed her walks and conversation with him. He told her about her brothers and sisters when they were little, and so much about Thomas. She knew Uncle Hugh had had an invalid wife who had died during the war; she had been stricken with a dreadful illness soon after they were married. She learned a lot from him and could understand her mother's deep affection for this old, old friend who was also held in high esteem by dear Mrs P and Stony and Boxer.

Nevertheless she was surprised when her mother and her new-found uncle announced their plans to marry. But the more she thought about it the more she was pleased. Hugh Neale was a fine man, her mother was the dearest of women – not a bit old like many mothers – still with her lovely colouring, girlish figure and bright and cheerful disposition. Her mother should have this second chance at a happy marriage, and they were pleased with her acceptance of their plans.

Hugh would be going up to Scotland after his holiday. There he would look for a house for them and when all was ready for their future life together he would come back to the Dower House, marry his dearest Polly and off they'd go to the wilds of Scotland.

Jet wouldn't let herself think of what it would be like alone without her mother, but her mother deserved this happiness. For herself she would have a busy life; there was the house to care for, the children to be educated, and there was the waiting for Thomas. Life wouldn't begin again for many 'until the boys came home'.

And then suddenly their prayers were answered: the war *was* over. Peace came like a bolt from the blue. One moment the village was hushed, quiet, as if in mourning, and the next people were rushing about, banging doors, blowing whistles, screaming, shouting; dogs were barking, babies crying. Everyone was hugging everyone else, laughing, talking, no one listening to anything except the magic words, 'It's Over'.

And who organised the concerted march to the top of Brandon Hill to light the beacon fire? Who laid it even, and when? In the distance could be seen fires from other villages, and bobbing lights from the torches carried by the long snaking line of mysterious human beings, onward and upward it coiled to the furnace on the top of the hill.

The world and his wife were out on this night of all nights. Nurses from the hospital with their blue-clad patients, on crutches, in wheel chairs. Everyone kissed everyone else. Jet felt she'd burst with happiness. The waiting was over, Thomas was safe, he'd be coming home.

There was of course a reaction after such a burst of human emotion. Memories of the men who made it possible. Sadness in the midst of joy, a guilty feeling at the uninhibited exhibition of released tension.

The Reverend Tozer held his Thanksgiving Service the next day. The congregation turned their thoughts to the men who would not see their children again; to the children of Great Little Tisbury who would not now be born; to the widows; and to the wives who would bear the burden of crippled husbands and sons. In the village lived a veteran of the Boer War. One wooden leg, a rough limb, like a piece hacked from a kitchen table. He had lived a hand-to-mouth existence on the parish, his clothes a tattered greatcoat held together by a safety pin.

Jet felt the tears burn her eyes as the veteran, Tom Sutton, tapped his way into the church. Today his medals were pinned to his greatcoat. He stood, holding the back of the pew in front of him, chest out proudly. What had Great Little Tisbury done for this one hero returning from his war? 'Lest we Forget.' Jet knelt down and cried, muffling her sobs in her scarf.

Then the Reverend Tozer asked them to be silent and remember the dead and the maimed. Obediently they bowed their heads; the church had never been so full, or so silent even when empty. But the birds still sang outside.

In the stillness and silence of the church there came a half-stifled groan from the back of the church. Jet's skin went tight. She shivered. Everyone turned. Helen Fraser, the matron from the hospital, was helping Amelia to the door. She had been heavy with child, the birth imminent, but had insisted on coming to the Thanksgiving and Memorial Service.

The Reverend Tozer chalked up another invisible demerit mark against Amelia Harvey, *née* Fox. For the first time he had had a congregation in the palm of his hand. A deliberate diversion on Amelia's part, he was sure.

James, already alerted by a swift messenger was ready for Amelia, he had hot water, and every emergency was planned for. There were two maids to fetch and carry, and the matron of the hospital, an unexpected guest, was an experienced assistant. Thus on a day of peace and thanksgiving Amelia's son was born, noisily and hungrily it seemed, for he was chewing his fist.

'Hush darling,' said Amelia as the baby yelled. 'Your mama has already spoiled the Reverend Ezekial's memorial speech, and he'll hear you from here. He'll have his revenge at your christening.' The baby stopped crying and James kissed Amelia.

But Ezekial's days were numbered, in Great Little Tisbury, that is. Mrs Ezekial Tozer, the delicate invalid, turned into a raging virago, just when the Reverend had heard that Absalom was not coming back to his church, just when the peace had spread a different spirit amongst his congregation, just when he could see (but only he) popularity for him ahead.

Veronica Tozer was still, in public, the delicate martyr. 'It is the Lord's will', she acted permanently. Behind the scenes, only to Ezekial, did she show her true self. A cold woman, she had taken to her invalid way of life as an excuse and release from her 'dear husband's loving advances'. He considered them his 'right by holy wedlock'. Now she wanted release from the Rectory too, and sadly and quietly informed the Bishop of her husband's 'extra-marital activities' in the direction of the Widow Starkey.

Mrs Tozer had become friedly with Miss Wash, intending to take supremacy over Miss Tremlett in the affections of the lady draper. Veronica wasn't without money, that was something she had managed to keep Ezekial's hands from (besides other things). She had watched, waited, and listened. Now she struck, just when she knew her husband thought he was settled for live in the lovely Rectory.

However, to give Tozer his due (or it may be that the flesh was more willing than the spirit) he did his duty by the widow. Overnight he and the lady disappeared from the village and the delicate Mrs Tozer moved in with Miss Wash. 'My partner' was how Emmeline introduced Veronica to the travellers. Almost overnight it seemed, the delicate Mrs T regained her health and strength, a miracle for Emmeline and Veronica, but a sad disappointment for Miss Tremlett.

At the Dower House Polly and Jet and Mrs P were putting the finishing touches to the spring-cleaned welcome prepared for Thomas. Prisoners of war had been arriving home and Thomas was expected at any time. 'Today?' they always hoped on rising.

Jet was in the garden. The school was on holiday. What flowers should she put in Thomas's rooms? Polly and Mrs P were chatting to her from an upstairs window when Boxer arrived with a telegram. Jet grabbed it from him as he shouted 'It's not for 'ee, Jet, 'ee mustn't open it,' but it was too late. Jet stared up at her mother as the opened wire fluttered on to the flowers which had dropped from her arms, and as she swayed Boxer caught her, yelling for his brother.

As the two women rushed out into the garden Polly grumbled to her friend, 'I knew she'd be like this. It's no good telling her to keep calm. I hoped she'd grow out of this excitement when Thomas came back from anywhere.'

'Oh Poll, it's different this time. All these years he could have been killed in the war. She'll be all right, just a bit of giddiness.'

But it was more than 'just a bit of giddiness' for Jet was in a deep faint. Stony sent his brother back to the village for Dr Harvey while Polly and Mrs P tried to revive her. Stony told his wife what had been in the wire and it was left to a tearful Mrs P to tell Polly that her first-born was dead.

'Oh God, oh God, that you can be so cruel, just now

106

when we thought we'd only lost our Wheel.' As Jet stirred on the sofa Polly said, 'Jet, Jet, Mam's here. Come on Jet, look at Mam.' Jet opened her eyes. She looked sleepy and somehow dazed. 'Mam'll make a nice cup of tea.'

'I'll make it.' Mrs P was anxious to get away for a minute. It was too much for her to cope with. The dreadful news had started her tears. She was remembering times past. The pain in Polly's eyes as she spoke in a cheerful soothing voice to Jet, the strange look about Jet. 'Thank God I never had no bairns.' She was sure she could never have stood up to things like 'young Poll'.

Dr Harvey came. He'd heard the news from Boxer. He appeared quite casual. He gave Jet a sleeping draught and seemed more concerned with Polly. He was, however, worried when he spoke to Amelia that evening.

'I hope Jet remembers all the pain when she wakes up for, if she has amnesia, it'll be a long journey for her back to reality.'

But Jet did remember when she woke up. She appeared quiet and calm when James Harvey came in the morning. He invited Polly and Jet to dinner the next evening. Everyone was trying to act as usual and not concentrate on the dreadful tragedy if they could help it.

Jet seemed to behave normally as the days went on, but Polly knew her own daughter. She knew Jet was fighting to retain her strength to face the future. She never mentioned Thomas. She was studying again as though she would re-apply for Somerville, but she never mentioned it.

Polly wondered, not for the first time, if she would ever wed Hugh. They were fated. How could she leave

107

Jet and go across the country to Hugh? He said he would leave his job as soon as he could and try for even a farm labourer's work in Great Little Tisbury to be with them. But Polly would never let him sacrifice his career. She knew how deep was his love for his work.

However, Jet solved the problem for her mother. In spite of the coldness within she was still an unselfish girl. She was grateful to her mother for her happy childhood and love, and wanted so much for Hugh to be married to her.

In the end she told Father Shields the whole story. The new rector would have caused a stir in any village community, but after the thin, miserable Tozer, he was a lovely gift. A plump jolly parson with a plump jolly wife and six plump jolly children. He and his wife, Kathleen, were so similar that they looked like brother and sister and the three boys and three girls looked like younger brothers and sisters.

Father Shields, as he was affectionately known, was a man of substance in more ways than one. His three boys had been entered from birth for a famous public school. The three girls had a nanny and a governess. It was quite a sight to see the Shields household file into church on Sunday morning. They filled two pews kept reserved for them. Mrs Shields beamed at the congregation, the congregation almost smiled back, and the singing of the Shields family and staff added greatly to the volume of sound, if not the quality. The little girls' stockings were always wrinkled round their legs.

Stony called Father Shields, 'The Roly-Poly Vicar with his six Dumplings'. After the depressing years of war, the Shields were just what the village needed, fresh, booming life. Father John's brother Herbert was Professor of Agriculture and Botany. The Dymchester

Red Cross hospital had closed and it had been decided to turn it into a college of agriculture. The wartime shortage of food had stimulated a desire to improve the output of the land. Professor Shields would be Head of the College.

Father John approached his brother at the moment when Herbert Shields was planning his staff. Hugh was invited to apply for the post of Forest Manager and he was successful. He was given a house in the college grounds. It had formerly been used for stores and would need some work on it, but this did not present a problem, for Polly and Hugh had accommodation at the Dower house.

So they would be married at last in the village church. A quiet wedding, they thought at their age, and after all that had gone before. Mrs P, however, had a talk with Jet. She told her of the evening when she and Polly had found a wedding dress in the trunk upstairs. How the children had laughed at their mam's blue and white spotted wedding dress and how Judy had turned up her nose at the gown they'd taken from the trunk.

'I'll never forget how your mam looked when she put the gown away, Jet. Wouldn't it be lovely if she could wear it after all? Remember how everyone admired it on Miss Fox?

'Oh that gown; it was absolutely beautiful, but then Amelia is short and mother is tall. I don't think mother is bigger otherwise, is she?'

'No Jet. When we got it back we took the hem and sleeves down again. Mrs Harvey wouldn't allow us to cut the material. She said it was too beautiful, someone else could wear it. What do you think?'

'I think you might have an argument with Mam. She'll say she's too old and that, but if you can get it to fit I think it would make her day. Don't let her know

109

you've told me. I think I'll surprise Mam and Uncle Hugh. I'll get Miss Wash to play the organ.' But after her enthusiasm Jet sighed. 'At least it will be a fresh start in life for Mam and Uncle Hugh.'

'Oh you poor old thing,' laughed Mrs P. 'You're young, Jet; you won't always bear this burden of sorrow.' She wasn't sure as she said it whether she believed it herself. Jet was different.

After much cajoling, almost bullying on Mrs P's part, Polly gave way and wore the beautiful antique wedding gown. She had become slim since her two sons were killed, and she'd been worried about Jet. Meg's fiancée, the Hubbard boy, had also been a prisoner of war and although Meg was out of sight she wasn't out of Polly's mind, especially after the tragedy of Thomas, for he'd been safe as a prisoner of war they had thought.

Judy was in a play and wouldn't be able to come down for the wedding but she sent them a beautiful eiderdown and cover. Polly was overjoyed with it. Judy also sent some money to Jet for her mother's wedding bouquet, which was to be a surprise. Jet didn't know what to give for her present; then she remembered the photo of the family. Jet didn't know it had been taken for Hugh after she was born, but there they were, all the Brights. Polly was sitting in a velvet chair, baby Bridget on her lap. At her feet were the twins. On either side gazing at the baby were Meg and Judy. Thomas was leaning over his mother's shoulder.

Jet took this to Dymchester and arranged for the photographer to make an enlargement. He suggested an artist to colour it and Jet gave him particulars of the family for this purpose. She also arranged for the photographer to be at the church to photograph the bride and groom. Worried that the colouring of the

110

family photograph might be too vivid, she ordered sepia copies as well. Then to the jewellers for silver frames. She felt happier than she had done for some time for she knew her mother would treasure the photographs.

Polly's rose bouquet was rich cream and peach, the blooms choice. The miniature lace headscarf and parchment silk dress were perfect foils for the shining copper coils of her hair. Jet could not remember her mother's smile so radiant as, watched by her friends and family, she came back down the church as Mrs Hugh Neale. Olive Tremlett wiped away her tears. 'Dear Polly, she deserves this happy day. I think the organ has made me cry.'

Amelia and James had given the bridal pair a different sort of wedding present, luncheon at the Bull Hotel, and so this quiet event became the joyous wedding the couple deserved. Miss Wash and Miss Tremlett sat happily side by side, Mrs Tozer not, of course, being one of the intimate circle. All Polly's friends were there, in addition to some of her family.

Emily had made and decorated the cake. Wally had given his mother away, announcing that he and Emily would be the next Brights to be married. The guests smiled for Emily was a Newbold. Hugh gave a speech thanking his best man, James Harvey, and toasted absent friends, Absalom, Angcla and family, Judy and Meg and Bessie. Bert Porlock sang a song and surprised everyone with his lovely baritone.

And Hugh kissed the bridesmaid. Jet. A surprise between Mrs P and Jet for Polly. They had found, at Miss Wash's, some pretty gentian blue georgette with a tiny white spot. Miss Wash made Jet the dress and she wore a straw hat with the same material round it. Polly thought it all too marvellous; she didn't deserve such love and thoughtfulness and she was beside herself with excitement some time later when the silver-framed photographs arrived.

Back at the Dower House in the evening, Polly and Hugh sat round the sitting-room fire. Jet had gone to make coffee.

'Polly, dearest, I don't think we should put off the fateful day any longer. Let us start our marriage by telling Jet what she should know.'

'What should I know Uncle Hugh? Sorry. Father Neale; that sounds a bit religious, doesn't it? I'm old enough to call you Hugh. That's all right isn't it, Mother?'

Polly looked worried and Hugh said, 'Pour the coffee, dear, and your mother and I will talk to you but your mother is afraid much of what we have to say will be too upsetting for you. I think we should risk that, Jet, for all our sakes. It is better that your mother and I tell you than you risk being told by someone else. I am relieved you have never learned all this before. I do not think what we have to say, Jet, even if it upsets you, is anything to make you suffer'.

Polly spoke of the time before Jet was born. She had been a young widow with five young children to support. She was living and working as a caretaker at the Dower House, managing on the money she obtained for work she was able to do. She had good friends and relations but money was not plentiful anywhere then and everyone had a life of hardship in the country. Her husband had been drowned at sea and she received a little help from Grandmother Bright, but it seemed salvation was at hand when the Hall asked her to give lodgings to the forester who would be coming to reorganise the estate.

In the end she and Hugh had fallen deeply in love,

resisting temptation for a long, long time, as Hugh's beloved wife was in an asylum and he was true to his wedding vows. One evening, however, they'd been to a magnificent ball, the first time Polly had seen such wonders and it was that night she and Hugh had become man and wife in their love for one another.

Hugh had worked round the country and had even gone abroad to obtain the highest wages possible so that after he had supported his wife he might send some money to his dear Polly and beloved daughter.

Hugh took Polly's hand as she finished talking. As he drew it to his lips Jet came forward and kissed them both.

'I wonder I haven't guessed before. Judy would say I am naive. After all, I can see I have your eyes and your expression. And I am very sorry you will be going away again.'

Jet was surprised to find Polly had more to disclose. Hugh knew she would find her confession about Thomas a little difficult if he was there and he went off to the kitchen to prepare a light repast for his two ladies.

Polly told Jet of the funny little 13-year-old she had been the day she came to the Dower House seeking work as a maid for Lady Margaret Brensham. Her father had died the day before, money was short, and she was decked out in second-hand clothes, none suitable for a child of 13.

Polly spoke with pride of her success in obtaining this good situation, of the kindness of her employer, which was unusual, and it was obvious she loved the Lady Margaret. Dominic, her ladyship's grandson, was also 13 and his school holidays were spent with his grandmother. He and Polly, the only two young things about, were together a lot, class was forgotten.

One day when they were just in their teens Polly went blackberrying. It was Dominic's last day before going on to college and he'd see young Polly no more. His future holidays would be spent abroad, skiing, travelling, as befitted a future aristocrat. Dominic decided to help Polly with the blackberrying. They teased each other and laughed and had fun picking the berries. Dominic decided to go round the bend of the river, out of sight of Polly, and swim. It was a sweltering hot day and they'd got hot and sticky.

Polly decided she wouldn't be seen if she took a dip in the river on the other side from Dominic. It was nearly a tragedy for her foot caught in the weeds. When Dominic finally rescued her she was unconscious. He thought she'd drowned.

Polly, over the years, had found it difficult to believe, herself, that Thomas had been conceived in that truly loving incident after her rescue from drowning. How could she convince Jet that what had happened in that hot summer meadow to two young people, for the first time in their lives, was due to relief that she still had life instead of death, radiant joy after sheer, stark terror?

'He went to college, No one guessed I was expecting except Philip Bright, who knew before he married me. It was just the once, you see Jet, an accident really, a terrible happening. But it seems Lady Margaret must have guessed.'

At last Jet spoke. 'I can understand being only a half-sister to Meg and the others but I am sad that I wasn't a whole sister to Thomas. In a way it is as though I shouldn't have taken ownership of him as a sister, for I realise now that is what I did. I gave him all my love, and I was only half related to him. Did Thomas know?'

'Yes, Thomas knew, but Hugh had to go away. Thomas took care of you and loved you, Jet; he never

114

looked on you as a half-sister.' Polly looked a bit tearful.

Jet leapt up. 'Oh Mum, it's not for me to judge; I've no right. I must thank you not only for you but for the father you've given me'.

Jet closed her eyes and thought of Thomas. So he knew before he went away that they were only half-brother and sister. He also knew that the house they both loved would be his one day. What did he say? 'Goodbye Jet; take care of *our* house; keep it safe for *us* and for me to come home to.' She admired her mother for telling Thomas before he left. Knowing he was going to war it was very brave for he might have left her in anger.

'Anger?' No, not Thomas. It was that thought which brought Jet back to considering her mother's feelings. She thought of the little Polly Hilton coming to the Dower House for a job, in second-hand clothes, only 13 too. How hard she had struggled. What a good mother she had been, and love for this dearest of souls welled up within her.

'Mam, how worried you must have been over the years. How hard you have worked all you life. I am so glad you had a happy day today for you looked so beautiful.'

'Get away with you Jet,' laughed Polly. But she was touched. 'I'll put the dress away carefully Jet. It might make another bride as happy as Amelia and I are.'

'What about Meg, Mother?'

'Meg's trouble,' Polly sighed, 'is that she is big as well as tall. This gown can only be altered lengthwise. Pity; we'll get her one she'll love from Miss Wash, made to measure.'

Jet kissed her mother and they went off to supper. Hugh looked at them anxiously.

'It's all right, new father of mine, the skeletons are all out of the cupboard and they don't look too bad considering the time they have been locked up. Only one thing, Papa, I prefer my surname of Bright. Jet Neale sounds as though I have been kneeling in the dirt.'

Hugh laughed, 'I really think it's best for you to keep the name of Bright, which you were kindly given. One day you may have children and perhaps will call your son Neale, or have it joined on if you want to keep it in perpetuity.' Polly looked at Hugh with love, his words, his voice were as fine as his character.

'There is so much for me to think about,' said Jet.

'It has hardly all sunk in yet. I believe you said the house was to become Thomas's under Lady Brensham's Will. Would I be callous to ask if it reverts to the estate and shall we have to move at any time? I'm not worried, Mam, because I know I can live with a mother and a father now, or there's Amelia's cottage at the school she still owns, or perhaps I could pull my socks up and try hard for the Somerville entrance exam again. It's just that I wonder what is going to happen to Thomas's house, he and I loved it so.'

'Oh Jet, don't worry, Whatever will you think of me? When I intended to tell you all about the things you had to know I meant to give you Thomas's letter because it all goes with it. He left this here for you in the event he didn't come back.' Jet heard the lump in Polly's throat.

She got to her feet and kissed her mother and father. 'Good night now. I'm going to bring you tea in the morning and spoil you for a few days.'

Jet took the letters her mother handed her from her wooden box, the box inlaid with mother-of-pearl.

'There's also one that came from Thomas at his camp in Germany. I didn't give it to you before because it

116

came after he died and it would have upset you so.'

Jet took the letters up to Thomas's room to read. He always seemed so near to her there.

11 January 1915

My dear Jet,

You will see that this is a business-like letter. If you ever have to read it then it will be better this way. I know even now how you will be feeling when you read this; pray God you never have to.

Mother will by now have told you of the circumstances of my birth, and also of your birth. Your birth makes no difference to me for I have loved you dearly as a brother from the moment you were born and you were the dearest thing in my life.

Because of my birth I must put my affairs in order before I leave. Our house becomes my property on my 25th birthday and if I am unable to claim it I want you to have it for you love it as I do.

I do not want to be unfair to my brothers and sisters so I know you will keep the house as it is now, our home, for whenever it is needed.

Uncle Daniel says what he has will be for the twins and Judy will benefit from Grandmother Bright. Uncle Daniel added that if the war should keep on and the twins go then he would substitute Meg for the boys. You will understand all this now.

You will of course have my books etc. but any money I think should be for Meg, and of course anything from the house she may wish.

I know all you want to do having read this is to give up, but Jet you must go on. There is Mother to care for if Uncle Hugh cannot share his life with her.

There is also me, Jet, for I want you to do what you would have done had I returned. Don't let me

117

down; more importantly, don't let yourself down.
   All my love little sister,

Jet kissed Thomas's signature and she wept.

She opened the second letter she wished she hadn't received. Peace was in the air, the end of the war was in sight, the prisoners were reprieved. Joy was in the air, 'WE ARE COMING HOME!'

Jet wept again. She forced herself to read the rest of the letter. His dear friend and comrade Captain Peter Meredith would be coming to see her. He hadn't been captured, as Jet knew. Thomas had entrusted to him all Jet's letters and her precious war diary. Peter would be bringing them to her and Thomas thought he should warn her to be on her guard when she met Captain Meredith. She would be in for the shock of a lifetime.

Jet wouldn't let herself think of what had happened after this letter had been written. No, she didn't want to know. It wouldn't bring Thomas back. There had been an enquiry. Mass escape. Prisoners shot. Who would try to escape when the war was over?

Polly and Hugh went up to Plumstead for Meg's wedding. Well, Bessie's as well; they were marrying the Hubbard brothers. Jet would see them when they came to the Dower House which Jet had offered them for the honeymoon. The girls were delighted. They would be able to show off their new husbands to their relations and schoolfriends.

The Hubbard 'boys' were quiet, placid men, ideal life-partners for Meg and Bessie. The only time they appeared the least bit excited was when they were talking about the business they were starting 'with our dad up in Plumstead'. Dad was a bricklayer, Meg's husband Bert, a plumber, and Bessie's husband, a carpenter.

118

They said there was a lot of building going on 'up London' now. Jet was sure they would do well, equally sure they would all be happy together. Ma and Pa Hubbard had found the ideal accommodation for living and working in. A large bay-windowed residence on three floors, a pair of Hubbards on each floor.

Jet wasn't sure she would care for an *en masse* wedding, honeymoon and future. Lonely as she might appear to the rest of the world, Jet thought it infinitely worse never to be alone. The honeymooners had obviously had a wonderful time. They went back loaded with linen from Granny Bright's house. Meg said she didn't think Granny Bright would have liked it had she known Meg was having this lovely linen but Jet said Meg was Granny Bright's eldest grandchild. Who else was more entitled?

At this both Jet and Meg cried, remembering mother's first-born, Thomas.

'Our brother Thomas was lovely, Bert. If only you'd met him.' Meg took her husband's arm. He patted it awkwardly.

'It's the bloody war, mate,' he said. 'The good ones don't come back.'

Jet was touched at this gesture from Bert and was pleased they were delighted with gifts to take back. Home-cured ham and bacon from Polly and Mrs P, furniture from Granny Bright's and the Dower House; their van was loaded to capacity. Jet had a feeling that two weeks in the country, even though on honeymoon, had been enough for these London chaps for they were excited at going home. They were very keen for Jet to stay with them: 'You wanna see our big yard. It's got a workshop and office in it.' Jet promised she'd visit them if ever she went up to London (which she didn't think likely). Apparently Ma Hubbard was proud her sons

119

had found clean, hard-working country girls, better than the London sort!

Life for Jet settled down into a simple, if not unpleasant, routine. School during the day. Dinner with James and Amelia once a week, enjoyable discussions with Amelia when James was out. Lunch with Polly and Hugh on Sundays, dinner with them one evening a week. There was the parish council meeting once a month and sometimes she dined with the Shields at the Rectory.

Occasionally she wrote to Meg, to Judy, never. Judy was not much of a letter-writer and when she did write to her mother she would say, 'Remember me to Jet. I suppose she's still got her head stuck in a book.' Jet always said, 'Send Judy my love, Mum.'

She went for long walks with her newfound father. She learnt much about trees but also discovered what a fine man he was. He was serious but not miserable, and he was learning to relax for at last, in late-middle age, his burdens had been removed, burdens he'd borne patiently for so long the memories and effects of them would stay with him. At long last he had a wife to care for him and share his life, a wife who looked on the bright side and tried to bring happiness to others.

He recognised in Jet something of himself and hoped, if she fell in love, as surely she would one day, she would be fortunate in the outcome. He was proud of her intellect but a little concerned that she was unworldly, unambitious and unadventurous. He was glad she was studying again for Somerville and hoped she would be accepted there. Even if she came back to the Dower House, which seemed to have possessed her somehow, she would have had some years of wider experience.

120

The walks with her father helped Jet in a little way to bear the pain of Thomas's death. She admired her father for his strength of character and his compassion, and although she regretted her childhood without him she was grateful for his presence now and for his deep love for her mother.

Jet arrived home one evening to find a brown paper parcel on the front porch. Meg's postmark. She took it into the kitchen, put the kettle on for tea, and opened the parcel.

An untidy parcel. Out tumbled hundreds of sheets of paper and old envelopes. What ever could this be . . ? They were Jet's letters to Thomas during the war. Why did the parcel have Meg's postmark? She searched amongst the letters for a long time before she found a note from Meg. It read: 'Ever so sorry, Jet. Judy brought these when she came to our wedding. That captain friend of Thomas's gave them to her for you. She met him somewhere. Love to Mum, In haste, Meg.'

Jet bundled the letters in a drawer in the kitchen dresser. She'd burn them sometime. She felt depressed. She made the tea and cut some bread and butter. So much for Thomas's dear friend and army comrade, Captain Peter Meredith. The letters weren't even packed properly. She wondered how Judy had met this Peter Meredith. She decided she was glad he hadn't written or come to the country; she was sure she wouldn't have liked him. She wished Judy had mentioned to Polly that she'd met Thomas's friend. She wasn't cross that Meg had taken the letters from Judy, put them away and forgotten them. Meg was about to get married when Judy saw her. It was just like Judy to thrust them at her sister at such a time. Knowing Judy,

121

she was sure there was some reason for not despatching the letters direct. She puzzled for a long while, in the end dismissing the matter with a shrug of her shoulders. 'What does it matter? I shall burn them anyway.' But it did matter, Judy hadn't mentioned meeting Thomas's friend Peter in her last letter to Polly. Why not?

Three months later Polly received a letter from Judy

Dear Mother,

Am going to be married. Visiting in Hampshire for a few days. Will see you on the way back to London. Shall be staying at the Bull. Would like to give dinner to my friends at home so that they can meet my fiancée. He is looking forward to meeting you. Would Hugh book up for us at the Bull from the 11th to the 14th and book dinner for you and Hugh, Jet, Emily and Wally, the Harveys and Miss Wash. With us, that would make ten. We'll have a party. Would you ask all concerned to keep the 12th free, for the dinner with us. Hastily, Judy

Polly was very excited. 'Judy going to be married. That only leaves you Jet. You'll have to buck up, gel.' Jet had a sharp retort on her tongue, but she held it back.

'Why all the mystery? Nothing about the man, not even his name.'

'Oh, she wants to surprise us all. I bet he's clever and handsome.' Polly was sure Judy had made a catch.

'And rich,' added Jet.

'Well, why not?' Polly was on the defensive. 'When poverty comes in by the window, love flies out of the door.'

'Would you like me to go to the Bull, to save Hugh a journey?'. Jet was sorry she had been a wet blanket.

122

What *was* the matter with her?

'No thank you, luv; Hugh dashed off as soon as we got Judy's letter.' Again she felt irritated. 'I've asked him to call at Mizwash's for some books and patterns of material. I'll get her to make me a special frock for Judy's party. Hugh wants me to have blue.'

'It *is* your colour, Mam.'

'What will you wear, Jet?'

Jet felt that whatever she wore would look country cousin against Judy's fashionable gown. The thought of it made her want to go in her oldest frock.

'Oh, I'll find something in my wardrobe.'

'Oh Jet, you haven't had anything for ages. I can't remember when you bought anything new. You ought to try and look nice for your sister's party.'

In Jet's mood, Polly couldn't have said anything worse.

She went on. 'You live in the blouses and skirts you wear at school. You just screw your hair in a knot. It is such a pity. You know Mrs P used to say to me, "That's the young lady who pays for dressing. *She* could show 'em if she wished," and you could you know.' Polly looked cross.

Jet ignored this. 'It wouldn't have hurt Judy to have invited the Plumbs.'

Polly had been thinking this herself but she wouldn't let Jet know. Instead she remarked tartly, 'Judy knows the Plumbs wouldn't come if she asked them, they don't expect it. Judy will come up to see them when she comes to us, or I can invite them to tea when Judy and her young man visit us.'

'Damn,' said Jet to herself on the way home. 'I can't say or do anything without hurting someone's feelings. I must be nice to the children. I must smile when I dine out, greet the village people with charming politeness.

123

If I say the wrong thing or be a little irritable, people take me to task, Mother, Amelia, all of them. Now I'll have to dress up for the party Mother will think I'm trying to spoil the evening for Judy. It *would* be the fatted calf for Judy. There's something strange about the whole affair. This public showing of the fiancée. Why? For me, of course, and for me to meet him in front of others. Yes, that was it. Now, for what reason?' Jet couldn't think but she made up her mind to be on her guard whatever the surprise (or shock) Judy had in mind for her sister. A polite, 'How do you do?' to the prospective bridegroom; 'I wish you every happiness,' to Judy; perhaps 'congratulations' to the young man; then off to chat to someone else. Let her mother ask the usual personal questions.

'Miss Nosey Parker. Mind Yer Own Business, It's Mine. It's Mine. Cry Baby. Cry', she heard again Judy's childhood calls to her. As she put her bag on a chair she glanced at the photo of Thomas and almost heard him say, 'Forget it Jet. It was such a long time ago.' She went to the bookcase and turned the photograph face downwards. No one was going to make her feel guilty, not in her present mood. Judy knew Jet would aways help her if she ever needed it. Her home was still Judy's home at any time she wished. Jet knew Judy had always resented her and would never go out of her way to assist Jet. Jet always had to be wary, never sure of how Judy would react. She also knew that this state of affairs worried Judy not in the slightest.

On the evening before the dinner party Jet decided she *should* buy a new dress and so she rose at dawn and journeyed to Dymchester. She remembered the exclusive dress shop, an elegant establishment, only ever one gown in the window beside a beautiful vase of flowers with all the stylish accessories on display.

A chic assistant measured Jet with her eyes, led her into a thickly carpeted salon, furnished with gold chairs which had exceptionally thin legs. She brought some gowns for Jet's approval but they were velvet and satin and had a heavy matronly look about them. Jet left the shop quite disappointed. Well, that was it. She'd go home and sort out one of her old frocks; perhaps a flower, or some ribbon might improve its antique appearance. Better buy suitable accessories in town here rather than dash back to Miss Wash's Emporium and perhaps settle for something she would never like.

A few yards from the shop, deep in thought, someone said excitedly, 'Bridget Bright, what a surprise, and what are you doing here?' Mademoiselle François, Jet's old French teacher.

François Deuprez had always had a soft spot for Jet, one of the few scholarship pupils at the High School. Coming from a poor French family François' sympathy was always with the underdog. She was delighted when a scholarship girl proved herself mentally miles above those from well-off backgrounds. She resented bitterly the attitude that the poor were illiterate through a difference in quality, that the poor were born that way, a different animal in fact.

A clever girl, she'd worked hard to attain her present position but she knew that without her sister's help she might have gone on the streets, like Ginette had. The family had lived a hand-to-mouth existence in the slums of Paris.

In her teens Ginette had left home and become a prostitute. She was ambitious for her younger sister, determined she should be successful in a different environment; François was clever. By the time she was nine Ginette owned her own establishment. François was later sent away to a good boarding

125

school and then to college. Ginette was proud of her sister. Then Ginette retired and married the owner of a Paris nightclub. On his death she became a wealthy woman, and she was determined François, her only blood relation, the only person she had ever loved, should make a good marriage.

Ginette moved in the best Parisian circles and due to her ceaseless search, François had met and fallen in love with a wealthy young advocate. This was her last weekend at school before she left for Paris and marriage.

She was not sorry to leave England. She had made few friends but she remembered Bridget and her family. She'd met Polly Bright when she'd brought her young daughter for her interview. She liked Polly's warm friendliness and had gone to tea several times when she'd been coaching Bridget for the college entrance examinations. She remembered Judith, the beautiful child, the one with the shrewd ambition of her own sister Ginette. Such an unusual family, each member poles apart. And Thomas. Where did he spring from? She wondered about the departed Mr Bright.

She had been sorry when Bridget decided not to go to college, sure that she would remain buried in that little English village. Life would pass this promising young creature by.

'And how is your dear mother? . . . And your brothers and sisters? . . . And Thomas, what of him? Coming down from Oxford about now?'

'He died. He was shot by a prison guard after the war.' Jet couldn't stop her eyes watering, Mademoiselle had that warmth of personality.

'Ah,' thought Francois. 'So this is why there is a sad look about Bridget; it's not because of the life she has chosen, it's the loss of her beloved brother.'

'Come, you need refreshment. My flat is just around

126

the corner. I must give you my new address – I leave next week – then if you are ever in Paris, you must come and stay with me and my husband Marcel.'

Jet would have loved an hour's talk with Mademoiselle, it would have saved her a wasted day, but she explained why she was there and why she had to get home. She simply must find something to wear; it might need a lot of attention to make it presentable.

François looked at Jet. 'We are the same measurement, yes?' Jet nodded. 'Then come with me. Thanks to my beloved sister Ginette, tonight you will wear a Paris creation.'

Brooking no argument, she took Jet's arm and led her to a house a few yards along the road. A large red-brick bay-windowed house, ivy covered.

François' flat was on the second floor. She settled Jet in an armchair in the sitting-room.

'Take off your hat and coat. I shall not be a minute.'

She returned with two very large cardboard boxes. From one she removed layers of tissue paper, and then with a 'voila' and a sweep of the arms, like the dress shop assistant, she displayed the Paris creation. Jet gasped. The gown, long sleeved, with a flowing skirt, was of grey silk, classically simple, different from any of the gowns Jet had seen that day. From her pocket François took a necklace of crystal and two little ear-rings. She held the necklace to the neck of the gown.

Jet was surprised. Grey sounded elderly; a plain grey frock sounded like a nun's outfit, yet this, in heavy, expensive silk, with it's flowing lines, was a gown such as Jet had never imagined. François, pleased with the effect, drew from the box a grey crêpe de Chine petticoat, sheer stockings and a grey crêpe de Chine camiknicker set. The petticoat and the camiknickers had been hand embroidered.

'Now for the *pièce de résistance*,' announced François. From the other box emerged an evening cape. It was made of soft chamois silky grey velvet; it had a little mandarin collar of crystals, like the necklace. François threw open the skirt; it was lined with the same material as the gown. Before Jet could get her breath back, two more things emerged from the magic box, a little grey velvet bag with a crystal fastening, and a pair of grey silk shoes with tiny crystal buckles.

'They may not fit,' said François, 'but we will think of something. Yes?'

'No', said Jet firmly. 'It is all too beautiful. Suppose someone should spill something on the dress, or I get the skirt marked getting to the Bull?'

'My sister Ginette has so much money, she sends me clothes, too many, but to refuse would hurt her. If I say I gave the grey gown to a little English miss who looked so beautiful in it with her copper coloured hair, she will feel very important, and if I say the little English miss was my scholar who got to college, she will burst with pride. All I require for the dress, my dear Bridget, is that you promise to visit Marcel and me one day. *After* you have been to college? Yes?'

In a daze Jet said, 'Yes, Mademoiselle, one day,'

'What is this Mademoiselle? My name is François, if you please. Now what about this shock of hair. It is too bad of you to neglect it so; you have a great gift. You should be ashamed.'

François went to the door and called in a loud voice, 'Edith!' In few moments a middle-aged lady entered. Immaculately groomed, she spoke in the tones of the upper classes.

François quickly explained the position to her friend, an ex lady's maid who lived in the flat below. Edith smiled at Jet, came across and removed the hair pins from her hair.

'I can really make something of this. I'll fetch the special things my lady always used.'

'But I must go, François, it's fifteen miles to the Halt, and then a long way on to my house. Then I have to get ready and be at the Bull at 6.30.'

Edith returned and François spoke to her quietly while Jet feasted her eyes on all the beautiful things laid out before her; she lightly touched the grey silk gown.

'It's all settled, Bridget,' said Edith, as though she had known Jet for years. 'Well, we think it may be settled. While François prepares lunch – at least you'll have time for that – I have to go out, and I'll explain when I return.'

Jet thought it was all getting a little mysterious, if not out of hand. All she wanted to do was grab the boxes and run. It would be too bad, now that she had the gown and cloak, and was getting a little excited about the evening, if she was too late to enjoy it all.

Jet helped François prepare the lunch and just when it was ready Edith returned.

'Everything is arranged. My brother is chauffeur to Lord Charlbury. His Lordship is in London until next week. My brother is at a loose end this evening and will drive you to the Bull. He will call here for you at 5.30.' Jet couldn't take it all in, the two ladies were so excited. 'Frederick suggests we go too and have dinner downstairs at the Bull, François. He has done that before and says it would be nice, as you will be leaving us soon.'

'You see, Bridget,' said François, 'one's good turns have a way of coming back to one.'

While François tidied away after lunch, Edith took charge of Jet. She had brought with her innumerable bottles, bottles beautiful enough to be ornaments in themselves. She poured drops from three bottles into the warm bath and left Jet for about forty minutes. By this time she was out of the bath and dry and beautifully relaxed. Then her hair was shampooed with other various mysterious potions, and the bathroom was free for François to commence her preparations for the evening.

When Jet's hair was dry and combed, Edith brushed it with special brushes and spent some time 'polishing' it with special silk buffers. It was all so soothing, Jet nearly fell asleep.

Edith then went off to her flat to get ready for the evening and returned when Jet was dressed. François met her at the door and said, 'Très elegant.' Edith had looked after beautiful aristocratic ladies in her career but she thought this country girl would compare favourably with any of them.

Edith put on a smock and set to work on Jet's hair. Finally, when it was coiled on the crown of her head, she felt quite naked. Then Edith concentrated on Jet's face and neck. As Jet sat patiently through all this she began to feel sorry for the society ladies if it entailed so much before one evening's dinner. She thought the hours spent by François and Edith wasted for her and them and she decided to visit the cloakroom at the Bull and wash her face – after Edith and François had gone into dine, of course. She must appear grateful. But all this making up wasn't her; she was much happier in a jumper and skirt. It took her only half an hour to get ready for any event.

She really didn't recognise herself when her friends proudly conveyed her to the long mirror in François's bedroom. She was sure her changed appearance would spoil any conversation that evening; her friends and relatives would be shocked into silence. Edith's brother arrived with his Lordship's car and they set off. Edith sat with her brother and François with Jet.

François was silent. She was thinking of this beautiful girl opposite her. They were both from a working-class background, yet no two women could have been further apart. What would Bridget think if she knew of Ginette's life? She remembered, as a child, when Ginette had her 'establishment'. Their private apartments were through a passage door leading out to the salon (where the gentlemen conversed and drank with the 'ladies' before retiring with them to a private room). François was supposed to enter the house through a side door but sometimes if Ginette was out one of the girls would let her in the front door. She'd sit in the salon and the girls would make such a fuss of her, teasing her, looking at her school books and exclaiming, she was the cleverest pussy-cat in France.

They gave her *bon bons* to eat; there was always a huge box of candies and glacé fruits, brought by the gentlemen callers, with the wine and flowers. Everyone was so happy always; there was music, gaiety, and such warmth . . . until the day which resulted in her despatch to the convent. She was in the salon when a gentleman called to visit. He too had been sweet to the young François. Ginette had returned unexpectedly in time to hear him say that little François was a charming pussy and he hoped one day to see more of her when she left school and joined the ladies.

Ginette boxed her ears, the gentleman left hurriedly, the girls were very quiet, and François went away to school. She thought of Marcel, her husband to be. She would be happy with him. He knew of Ginette's former life, and it hadn't shocked him. François smiled; in this cold country she would have been looked upon as a leper. She thought this hypocritical. She'd heard of the way the English aristocracy lived. Edith, formerly a

131

lady's maid, was a fountain of information. Here it was all so secretive and furtive. She was glad to be going home. Edith was coming with her. Ginette would enjoy her company, hearing tales of the lords and ladies and the world-wide travelling Edith had experienced.

The car stopped outside the Bull Hotel.

'We'll say *au revoir* here, dear Bridget. We shall go to the dining-room, you to your party. You have my address, and I know you will write.'

Jet went into the foyer/lounge. Saturday night these days was a busy night at the Bull. Since the war it had become a popular place, especially at the weekends. From miles around people came to the Bull to dine and spend the evening. Transport was easier now, and plenty of people seemed to have cars.

Jet walked to the reception desk in the corner of the lounge. People, waiting for friends, always glanced towards the door at the arrival of a newcomer; this time they more than glanced, they stared. Edith smiled at François – they had paused on their way to the dining-room – to watch the progress of their 'protégé'. They were pleased with the sensation Jet was arousing, though they knew she was quite unaware of it.

'She reminds me somehow of Sister Dominique at the convent. Bridget has the same purity of countenance. God help the man who falls in love with her. And God help her if she falls in love with a man she cannot have. There'll be no other for her.' François shivered, they should have left Bridget alone.

Edith took her arm as her brother arrived: 'Let's eat,' she said.

Edith's brother turned to speak to someone he knew and the two women paused again just as Jet reached the clerk at the counter. They saw a fair young man, who had been talking to the clerk, turn and look at Jet,

132

following the clerk's gaze. They saw his surprised stare, and they saw Jet's startled pause. It was all over in a flash and François wondered who was the young man who had disturbed Jet.

Jet *had* been momentarily startled. Shocked. She had thought, 'It's Thomas!' She regained her composure; she must pull herself together, she was getting obsessed. She had been to the Bull before, she was a local, and she was amused the clerk had not at first recognised her. The expensive evening cape, soft, silky, the grey against that unusual hair, the crystal collar twinkling green and grey, the wide grey eyes, the marvellous complexion.

Jet said, 'Don't you know me, John, in my Sunday best?'

He blushed and then he laughed, 'Cor, Miss, I'm ever so sorry. I'll take you up. The Doctor and Mrs Harvey have just gone up; they asked if you'd arrived. Your mum and the rest of them are there; you'll be the last.' He was thinking what a shock she'd be to the others. He couldn't think what had happened to the village schoolmistress.

He took Jet to the private room on the first floor, a lovely room, with a grand piano. He had been at school with Jet's brothers and sisters. What a family! He decided, in a moment of fun, to make an entrance, Jet Bright deserved it. He'd play his part. He opened the door of the room, and announced, 'Miss Bridget Bright'. There was a stunned silence. The clerk said, 'May I take your cape, Miss Bright?' Jet smiled and slipped off the cape. The gown was as startling in its elegance as the cape had been.

Bridget too, was startled, but kept her composure. So *this* was Judy's shock for her; the fair young man by her sister's side was the fair young man at the reception desk. The one she'd thought – for a moment only – was

133

her beloved brother.

She walked across to Judy, kissed her lightly, and said, 'So this is the lucky man. We have already met.' That would be one in the eye for Judy. She wasn't prepared for the shock which followed but managed to retain her polite smile.

'We have indeed,' said the young man warmly, 'I'm Peter Meredith, dear Thomas's friend.'

'How interesting.' Jet kissed Judy on the cheek. 'I wish you both every happiness.' She knew it was the last thing she wished Judy. 'Now I must say hallo to the others.'

She walked across the room, her mind seething.

Jet had been right in thinking that her changed appearance would spoil any interesting conversation. Hugh said Jet was the most outstanding woman in the room and Polly wanted to know how this transformation had happened. James said that her ensemble made all the other ladies appear overdressed, with which Amelia agreed. Even Judy, the beautiful, looked theatrical against her sister, too heavily made up somehow, yet before Jet's entry Amelia had been impressed again by Judy's vivid appearance. Judy's frock was a bright blue and now its lace flounces looked fussy.

Judy had arranged the seating and had placed her sister at the opposite end of the table to herself and Peter. Miss Wash was on one side of her, Wally on the other.

'Wouldn't Granny Hilton and the Plumbs have loved all this,' Jet whispered to her brother.

'I don't thinks so Jet. Emily and I only came because Mam wanted us to. You know our Judy; she'll go round to Gran's tomorrow, and the Plumbs, loaded with flowers and things and they'll be just as pleased. They'd have had to get all dressed up. Uncle Daniel was glad

134

he'd be away at that wood auction. Wish I could have gone with him.'

Jet smiled, perhaps Judy knew her relations better after all. Miss Wash was very interested in the source of Jet's clothes.

'Paris,' said Jet casually.

'I thought so', said Emmeline, which amused her for Miss Wash had spoken so casually and Jet knew she would love to examine the garments thoroughly, the first she had ever seen from that great capital of fashion.

Jet could sense that Peter Meredith was aware of her during dinner. Judy was aware of this too, and extra watchful. She had guessed how Jet would react on meeting Peter because of the resemblance between him and their brother Thomas. This resemblance was uncanny. It disappeared when one began to speak to Peter. The likeness was there at the first meeting and then it came only occasionally in flashes. That wasn't why Judy wanted Peter, but only why Judy knew Jet shouldn't meet him until he was Judy's. It was lucky how they had met. Peter had written to Polly and explained why he had Thomas's correspondence. He asked if it would be possible for them to meet, or was it too soon after Thomas's tragic death for them to be able to talk about him?

Hugh wrote back to Peter on behalf of Polly and Jet. It was at the time when there had been such an upheaval. Jet had to be told about the true relationship between Thomas and his family, then her true parentage. There was Polly's wedding, Meg's wedding and Jet's future to be decided. Hugh and Polly thought it better to leave Peter Meredith's meeting or correspondence for a while, until Jet was well on the way to a new future. They wrote to Peter and gave him

135

Judy's address and also mentioned that she had her first part in a West End play. He might see her at the theatre.

Polly thought of no reason to tell Jet of this. After all Judy would write and send her letters to Thomas back although Jet had never suggested she wanted them. Polly thought the later they came, or indeed if they never came, the better.

So Peter went to see Judy at the theatre. The timing couldn't have been better. Judy, the young, the beautiful, with so much promise. Peter, well connected, educated, a young playwright with brilliant potential, only son of wealthy and doting parents. For Judy life was getting a little complicated; she and Gerald Davies, her actor/manager, were deeply in love. He was married and at that moment his wife was not suspicious.

Peter had just returned from a bloody war, his best friend and many comrades had suffered cruel death. Here was escape to sanity and cultured civilisation, to beautiful Judith Bright, warm, loving and feminine. The theatre was also his chosen world. It would be a perfect match.

Judy was quite aware that intellectually she and Peter were in different worlds but that mattered not a jot. She was ambitious; they would go places together in the theatrical world, and would be helping each other. She didn't think for a moment that when she took Peter to meet her mother and family he would fall out of love with her and fall in love with Jet. To her Jet was serious, insipid, prim, and dull in the way that a teacher can be, but she knew that Jet was well read and her type of conversation would be interesting to Peter from a literary point of view. Also he thought highly of the letters and diary Jet had sent Thomas, very highly;

136

he wanted to meet the writer.

Also Judy had a chip on her shoulder about Jet, stemming from childhood. Jet had not only usurped Judy's position as Mam's baby but had taken over big brother Thomas completely. They spoke the same language. Jet, so Judy believed, had always coveted what Judy had. She would cover Peter, Judy's ideal partner. Of course she would; he had been a friend of Thomas, he was attractive, clever, rich, perfect for any young lady. Judy thought herself the more attractive but she wasn't taking any chances until they were married. She'd keep her Peter under wraps. A fleeting visit to Great Little Tisbury would be in order. Judy had no idea she was or always had been jealous of Jet. They were just two different creatures, incompatible.

But Judy hadn't seen Jet for so long. She'd never seen the Jet who came to the party late and made an entry worthy of Judy's beloved theatre. She watched Peter talking to Jet, his eyes had strayed down the end of the table where Jet sat, during the meal. Now the guests chatted in twos and threes. Something warned Judy. She must take charge. Peter must come back to her side.

She went over to Miss Wash.

'Emmeline, you haven't heard me sing since my professional training began and, since you were the means of helping me in the very beginning, I would like your opinion of my voice now please.' Miss Wash looked very pleased and flattered. Judy clapped her hands. Everyone stopped talking. 'Emmeline would like to hear me sing. . ., if the rest of you can bear it,' Judy laughed modestly. They all clapped.

She played for herself and as she sang Jet watched Peter's face. He was absorbed. Jet leant her head back against her chair and closed her eyes. She let the magic

137

of the music and Judy's magnetic voice seep into her. The song was a sad one. As always, Judy was mistress of an audience's emotions. Jet was a child again playing in the buttercup meadows. She was riding on Wheel's shoulders. Wheel fell and she tumbled off into the sweet-scented carpet. She was waiting in the lane for darling Thomas to come home from school so he could give her a ride on the handlebars of the large old bicycle.

Jet felt the tears well up in her eyes and one slowly escape and trickle down her cheek. She made no attempt to wipe it away. Peter glanced at her, saw the teardrop slowly fall. It was like a drop of dew on a peach in the early morn. She had been charmingly polite to him, an aloof, reserved woman, he thought. Mistress of any situation. But as he watched her now he wanted to take her in his arms and comfort her.

As Judy's song ended, he too came back to reality. 'I am mad,' he thought. 'Bridget would never have had me, that is obvious. In any case, what am I thinking of? I am in love with Judith, of course I am.'

As the song ended the company applauded. Even though Judy's family and friends thought their Judy the most beautiful and wonderful of singers, the sadness of the song had affected them and so, in the midst of the applause, Peter went to the piano.

'Judith, I thought tonight was a happy occasion. No more mournful songs. We should be celebrating.'

Jet opened her eyes and saw them smiling together. She knew that once again Judy had something she, Jet, wanted. She knew that, as of old, whatever thing Judy had hold of she really possessed. This time it was different; this time she couldn't cry, 'I'm only looking, Judy.' This time Judy mustn't know; this time no one must know.

Tomorrow was Sunday, the day she lunched with her mother and Hugh. Judy and Peter were to be there for Peter to meet the Plumbs. She wouldn't go; a headache was quite feasible after an evening like this. They'd had wine; Polly knew that sometimes wine gave Jet a headache. She felt guilty about what had happened to her. She would write to Judy when she and Peter had returned to London. She'd wish them every happiness and success for the future.

But she did lunch with her mother on Sunday after all. Judy had decided she and Peter should return to London. She arranged, secretly, for Gerald to telephone early on Sunday morning with news that rehearsals for the new play had been put forward. 'Thank God for the telephone,' was Judy's first thought when she got Gerald out of bed late on Saturday night.

'Who was that this time of night?' was Gerald's wife's sleepy enquiry.

'Go back to sleep; it was a wrong number.' Gerald loved his protégé. He had turned her from a sullen country girl into this promising actress. Now he couldn't imagine his life without her.

Jet thought her mother would be very disappointed at Judy's hasty return to London, but she didn't appear to be even the slightest put out. She praised Judy for having sent flowers and chocolates to Mrs P and Granny Hilton, who apparently were over the moon at her thoughtfulness and remembrance of them. She was sending them photos of herself in a new musical, together with posters advertising the show. She even sent Stony and Boxer packets of their favourite tobacco.

Polly was excited when she told Jet that Peter was very interested in the war-time letters Jet had written to Thomas, and also her war-time diary. He now had a wonderful idea for a play based on the letters and the diary. Here her father took up the story.

'Peter Meredith said that although the diary and letters represented a journey's ending, in a way they could be a beginning also.'

Jet had no idea what this meant. How could the end of a journey be its beginning? Perhaps Hugh had got it wrong. Anyway she supposed playwrights looked at things in a different way from ordinary mortals. Polly said Peter would be down again at some time as he might need Jet's help to fill out some of the diary or letters.

'I *was* surprised to see the likeness between Peter and Thomas, weren't you, Mam?'

Polly turned to Hugh. 'I didn't notice it; what about you, Hugh?'

Hugh thought that there wasn't a strong likeness. Of course they were both slim, tall, fair and distinguished looking. Perhaps the lighting in the Bull had played tricks with Jet's imagination. After all, Peter had been Thomas's war-time comrade. Jet would have had Thomas strongly in mind when she met Peter.

'Perhaps that was it,' agreed Jet but her heart leapt at the mention of the two names, Peter and Thomas.

'No news of Judy's wedding. She sends you her love, Jet. It's three months since the party at the Bull. We thought she was getting married quickly. She said there was no need to wait. Don't you think it's funny?'

'No, I expect they are both too busy. I can imagine what it's like in the theatrical world.'

Jet had met her mother in the village for Polly had been to help Stony and his brother Boxer settle in the tiny cottage Father Shields had obtained for them. They would do bits of gardening and odd jobs at the

Rectory. Father Shields was a kindly Rector.

Both mother and daughter appeared depressed, both trying to think of Judy's wedding as a verbal distraction to take their minds off another family loss. More than a family loss, it seemed, for Mrs P had been part of Polly's life for so long and always part of Jet's.

When, after the war, a 'flu epidemic swept the country, taking with it many of its elderly citizens as well as other weakly inhabitants, Mrs Plumb had cared for, not only Stony and Boxer when they fell victim to the illness, but also her friends at the Halt. Polly also did what she could to help, and when the epidemic passed, or appeared to have passed, Mrs P became ill. Polly, Hugh and Jet took turns in the night watch at Stony's little cottage; Jet had taken Stony into the Dower house for he had only just recovered from his own illness. Mrs P received devoted nursing – James came frequently too – and it was tragic that Polly's dear friend should succumb when she had appeared to be the strongest of them all.

It was Jet's first experience of being with a dying person, someone she loved. She had to steel herself against weeping at Mrs P's bedside, especially when Mrs P said, 'I want you to have my amber necklace and brooch, Jet.'

'No, no, Plumb, you'll wear that yourself when you are better again.' Jet held Plumb's hand and did weep a little then.

Mrs P smiled. 'You always called me Plumb when you was a little 'un with those eyes, all solemn, and with that river of shinin' tresses.'

Just before dawn Polly's old friend died. She tried not to give way in front of Jet but it was no good, they were both distraught. Jet remembered Plumb bathing her knees after a childhood fall, Plumb singing her to

141

sleep, Plumb giving her dough for a gingerbread man, feeding the chickens with Plumb, searching in the meadow for the dark brown eggs from the little speckled bantam. Polly remembered a good friend, a friend who always supported her, a friend so loyal and so self sacrificing. She remembered the gown Mrs P had procured for her to go to the Ball . . . ah, that Ball, the night of her life, a glimpse of fairyland.

Polly said, 'We must help Stony now, for Mrs P, and mustn't break down again.' But at the reference to Stony, mother and daughter wept anew.

Jet felt nothing was predictable. Thomas, a prisoner, out of the war, yet killed by the enemy. Granny Hilton, old and frail, recovered from the 'flu without complications. Mrs P, strong and younger, nursing others to recovery, succumbed herself.

Amelia could see that Jet was getting into a rut and parochial. The life of the village seemed to be blinding her to all thoughts of what she had previously planned.

'There's no future here for someone like Bridget, James. Something must be done or else she'll turn into a miserable old maid of a village schoolmistress.'

'Well you didn't.' James kissed Amelia.

'I might have if you hadn't come along. No one will come along for Bridget, James. It's a pity Peter Meredith hasn't a brother. Judy's been a lucky young lady there.'

'I was watching them at the Bull, dear, and I thought for a moment that Peter's eyes were on Bridget in a strange manner. Couldn't blame him if he was attracted. Our Bridget was something different that evening, wasn't she?'

Amelia was horrified with her husband. 'Don't ever think such a thing, James. It would be too awful if Peter

142

had made a mistake and worse still if Jet thought of Judy's fiancée in a way that she shouldn't.' She tried to remember the evening at the Bull but all she could recall was the marvellous cape and gown Jet was wearing and the transformation in her appearance. She must have a talk with Jet. She was worried about her, she'd have to get her out of this narrow country life.

Amelia was convinced that Jet would stagnate without a chance for academic discussion and debate. Sometimes, although she was happy with James, she felt regret that she had not gone on to college. There was so much to be done for women, for the young. Throughout the land there were villages like this one, designating the disabled, without thought, as 'potential village idiots', villages lacking proper sanitation and telephonic communication, with the same old pre-war attitudes towards women and the poor, worlds apart from men and the ruling classes.

'If only a woman could have both worlds – family and a career – why does she have to choose?' Amelia determined Jet shouldn't stagnate.

Jet sat by the window in Thomas's room, it would always be his room for her. She gazed at the beautiful copper beech. She thought of Amelia's kindly advice. Of course she was right, there was nothing here for her now. There was no danger of the old pre-war tyrant of a teacher taking over now. There were too many guardians: Amelia, Father Shields, James, Hugh. Wonderful people. She wasn't needed now. What was she waiting for? Not Thomas. She would move on. She thanked Amelia. Had a strange premonition. 'Once I turn that corner I, too, will not return to this house.' She closed her eyes and saw again the dark figure against the red background. One arm raised in farewell. A wind seemed to race through the old

143

copper beech. The house stirred. A window slammed.

Jet shivered.

Things from then on moved too fast for her. Her acceptance by Somerville had been easy. She hadn't realised the extent of Amelia's co-operation and Miss Reynolds's battles on her behalf. Jet knew there was no going back, not this time.

She met the Head of the College at Dr Marjorie Reynolds's home, relieved that she was saved the journey of going to Oxford. She really was put through her paces, and was thrilled with herself that the interview was successful. It would be good at college. Nothing to do but study. A blessed retreat in a way, whatever Amelia thought. She was surprised with herself and quietly proud of her achievement, a little taken aback that everyone welcomed her decision. 'I'll not be missed,' she thought sadly. Polly and Hugh had not even demurred when Amelia had suggested selling the Dower House.

This hurt Jet. Never could she let the house go. Even if she felt fatalistic sometimes about her return, it was Thomas's house, it could not be sold. She would fret about it, it would be on her mind, it would be a betrayal. But no one would want to rent it, whereas Amelia and James would quite happily buy it. How could she pay her way at college without money? Oh why couldn't things be straightforward for her? Why all these problems? Why did it have to be expensive to attend a university, or so difficult?

Jet was cycling home from school, about five weeks before her departure for college. She had stayed behind to give some of her promising pupils this new term extra tuition for the scholarship examination. With the dusk there had come up an autumn mist. Approaching her house she glanced towards the bend.

Half hidden by the hedge, a yellow car appeared round the bend, suddenly leapt into the air, turned turtle and came down in a cloud of smoke.

Jet cycled quickly to the bend. The car seemed to be resting upside down in a small crater. There was dirt and oil everywhere. From a little space under the car, on the ground, Jet could see resting an arm and hand. She knelt down and peered underneath the car. Following the arm she saw the driver. Blood over his head and face, his neck appeared to be twisted. 'He's dead.' She was cross with herself at this reaction even though she felt it to be true. She remembered from somewhere that people in shock or illness must not be allowed to get cold. But how could she reach this man? Oh, but she could cover his arm and hand. She often woke with her hand and arm outside the bedclothes; they were frozen on the cold winter mornings.

She took off her coat and covered the arm and hand. She patted the hand and said, 'I'll get help, shan't be long'. She cycled off to Amelia's. Ether James or his partner would be there, she prayed. James was in. Jet poured out her news.

'Go to your uncle's, Jet. Tell him we want a stretcher and men'. James called to someone in his surgery. Then he shouted after Jet, 'Go home and get a bed ready downstairs in your house. Plenty of hot water, old clean sheets, light the fire.' Jet had already told James the driver of the car was dead. Hadn't he heard her?

She delivered the message to her uncle who left the shop to his wife and drove off in his car.

'You look done in, Jet. Shall I put the kettle on?' Bella hoped Jet wouldn't collapse before she'd done what James ordered.

Not waiting for the tea Jet cycled quickly home. She

145

did all that James had ordered. Lights on all over the house. Storm lanterns at either side of the drive entrance.

She didn't have long to wait. Along the garden path came a procession, James first, guiding four men who were carrying the injured (dead?) man on some hurdles from the farm. Amelia brought up the rear and Jet went into the kitchen at Amelia's request to bring hot water and clean clothes.

Amelia said, 'Keep the lights out in the lane, Jet. Your uncle's fetching a nurse from the cottage hospital with James's old friend the registrar.'

'Then the man's not . . .'

'Oh, he is alive, but only just. It will need a miracle, and we must watch and pray and do what we can. Doctors don't give up, fortunately.' She went off to help her husband, Jet went back into the kitchen to make tea.

She took fresh water and clothes into the sitting-room and brought out the bucket of used ones, trying not to think of the blood as she put them in the garden bin for burning. She had studiously avoided looking at the man on the divan. She stood by the kitchen sink; for a moment, there seemed nothing for her to do. She didn't want to think. The sight of blood had always made her faint. Another of Judy's taunts to her, 'Cowardy, cowardy custard'. It was somehow a relief to think of Judy at that moment, she seemed so normal. She would have made a good nurse, Judy; she'd not turn a hair at a wounded patient.

Jet heard the car and went to the door. A large efficient-looking woman strode into the house. Amelia came from the sitting-room, the woman went in, Amelia turned and shook hands with the man who now entered the house. She took him into the sitting-room

146

but a moment later she came out carrying the woman's outdoor clothes, a cape and a beret. Of course; she was the nurse.

'Will you prepare a tray for three, Jet. The nurse will come out for it.' Jet poured some tea for her uncle and Amelia which they drank standing up.

'Thank you for your help, Mr Hilton. I don't know what we would have done without you.' Amelia patted his shoulder.

'Glad to have been able to help the poor chap, Miss Amelia. (Even though Amelia was Mrs Harvey she was still known as 'Miss Amelia'.) Do you know who he is?' Jet's uncle seemed calm and dependable.

'You must be prepared for a shock.' Amelia looked quickly at Jet. 'It's Judith's fiancée Peter Meredith.' Jet dashed into the garden and Amelia could hear her vomiting. 'Oh God, I hope she's not going to be a problem. With things as they are here we have enough to cope with.'

'Oh Jet'll be all right, Miss. She's had a shock. She saw it happen, then she thought the man was dead, a stranger, bad enough; now he's just alive, only just, and it's someone her sister is going to marry.'

Jet's uncle was right. She fetched, carried, made tea, did as she was told, got out of the way, and waited. At last the nurse came and spoke to her.

'I shall be staying here with the patient tonight. Dr Harvey will be back again in an hour.'

'How is he?' whispered Jet. The nurse ignored her and took the tray she had prepared.

Amelia went off home with Uncle Albert. Jet felt lonely when they'd gone, but not for long. James came back with the doctor from the cottage hospital. Jet made them tea and sandwiches and gave them to the nurse. The doctor from the hospital went. James and

147

the nurse would be staying the night. What else should she do before she went to bed? Of course, the sitting-room fire must be kept alight. She went outside and filled two buckets. It was raining and she shivered in the night air. She came in and looked at herself in the kitchen mirror. It was cracked and gave one's face two parts. Wheel had cracked it with a catapult and Polly had worried about 'seven years bad luck'. She washed her hands and face and combed her hair.

What else could she do? She didn't want to sit down for then she would start to think. There was a tap on the kitchen door. James had returned. Amelia had been unable to contact Judith but had left a message with Gerald, who gave her the address of Peter's parents. They were on the way and would go to Amelia's.

'Could you rustle up some supper for Nurse Bottomley (Jet wondered what Christian name went with that surname) and I'll send her out in about fifteen minutes.'

Jet laid the table and grilled ham and eggs. She was cutting the bread and butter when the nurse came into the kitchen.

'There's a good girl. I shall enjoy this, but where is yours?'

'Oh I'm not hungry.' Jet couldn't have eaten a thing. She made coffee.

Nurse Bottomley looked at her. 'I shall want to know that you have eaten before you go to bed.' Jet felt like a naughty child.

'Now,' said the nurse, 'I shall go and wash and then, if you will make some sandwiches for the doctor for later on and leave the coffee ready, you can go to bed. I'll see to everything during the night.' Jet made some sandwiches and put the night trays ready. Obediently

148

she went upstairs. For a long time she sat on the top stair, ready to shoot into her mother's old bedroom if the sitting-room door opened. She didn't want to 'go to bed'; how could she with Peter lying there? Going to sleep was like opting out, removing her support, though she didn't see what support she had been. Anyone could have done what she had done. She recalled the expression of Amelia's when she, Jet, had been sick in the garden. Just for a moment it was there, that look of exasperation with human fraility. She could see Amelia and Nurse Bottomley tending the poor and the sick with their brisk business-like, no-nonsense manner. Fighting the enemy, had they been men, with vigour and delight. She would have been the soldier who fainted at bayonet practice. These women who succoured the weak, also despised the weak, or rather they designated which ones should be allowed a human weakness, which ones should not. For some reason or other her weakness would be a fall from grace; they would despise her.

The sitting-room door opened. Jet dashed into her mother's old room as Nurse Bottomley went into the kitchen. It was the same as it had been when her mother lived there. Hugh had brought new furniture for his bride. Jet had slept with her mother in the soft feather bed until she was five. She remembered the cold welcome from Judy when she finally transferred to being a 'big girl' and had a little iron bedstead in Judy's room. She missed her mother's soft warmth, holding her hand when she wasn't well, or woke up with 'the Lord Mayor'. She'd suffered a lot with nightmares when she was a child.

She undressed and sat by the window in her mother's old woollen dressing-gown. Her head was hot, and it ached a bit. She opened the window. The rain had stopped. The moist earth sent a strange perfume through the window. She bent forward to see the light from the sitting-room window. Like a beacon. Would it go out if Peter . . . She wouldn't think further. She felt shut out. 'You'll be absolutely no use here, my dear, go to bed.' Nurse Bottomley wouldn't have said that to Judy. How did these people know she could be ordered about, so soon after meeting her? There was plenty of chairs in the sitting-room, why couldn't she have shared the vigil with the nurse and James? They didn't know Peter. He belonged to Judy, there should be someone near him who loved him. In some mysterious way she felt she could have sent out a silent message to him in the strange between worlds, in which he was languishing.

'I'll go downstairs and creep quietly in to the room. I won't say anything, I'll just sit in the corner.' She got as far as the sitting-room door before she knew it was hopeless. One nod from the nurse's head and she would have been sunk. She wondered what Peter was doing when the car crashed; where had he been going? Perhaps to tell them of the wedding. Where was Judy when Peter needed her? At least she will be saved some hours of anguish; she won't know until it is all over.

The grey dawn was creeping over the top of the beech tree when Jet at last laid down on her mother's bed. She'd seen a falling star and it had made her shiver. She didn't intend to sleep but did indeed sleep heavily for she was woken by the sun shining across her face. For a moment she couldn't remember what had happened, then she felt guilty. 'Oh, I meant to be downstairs at dawn to take tea to James and the nurse.' She threw on her clothes and crept hurriedly downstairs. No sound from the sitting-room. All was well.

150

All was tidy in the kitchen. Cups and plates stacked ready for washing. Good, they'd had coffee and eaten the sandwiches. She screwed up her hair and tapped quietly at the sitting-room door. No one came. Plucking up courage she gently opened the door a little way. The empty bed made her heart jump. The sitting-room was untidy and empty. Where had they gone? Why hadn't she heard anything? Perhaps James had left a note. She searched. No. They might have said what had happened. She felt very angry. How could they frighten her like this? She looked at the clock; 'Good heavens, a quarter to nine, late for school. The children will be hanging about outside.' Without even waiting for a cup of tea, or washing, she threw on her coat and cycled furiously to the village school. No children in the playground, perhaps they'd all gone home.

She opened the schoolroom door. Amelia was sitting at Jet's desk talking to the children. She glanced at Jet, ordered the children to carry on reading, and took Jet into the kitchen. She thought Jet looked ghastly, dark smudges under her eyes, hair untidy.

'Have a wash, Bridget, comb your hair, and make yourself some tea. I can carry on here.' She knew Bridget needed sleep but more than that she needed a firm hand.

Jet burst out, 'They've gone. I kept awake all night and then just when I dozed off, they all left. Did Peter . . .?' Jet couldn't say the word.

'James has taken Peter to the cottage hospital. The ambulance came at first light. He is still unconscious, but alive. His parents are with him, and there's still no news from Judith, not that she could do anything. You have done your part.' Amelia nearly added, and now you must get on with your normal routine.

151

She was glad she hadn't said this for Jet washed and tidied herself, drank a cup of tea, ate two biscuits, and went out to take charge of her pupils.

'We'll make a strong woman of her yet,' Amelia thought as she went back to her home.

Hugh called for Jet after school that day.

'Your mother thought you'd like to have your evening meal with us, and perhaps stay the night. She didn't want you to be on your own with all this happening.'

Jet could have burst into tears; instead she said, 'But I have such a lot of clearing up to do. I can't leave it.' She knew what an effort it would be to see to that room – the stained clothes – but it would have to be done.

'Your mum and I have done it all. It was easier for us.'

Polly and Hugh fussed around Jet as though she was an invalid and Polly finally tucked her up in bed with a kiss.

'Have you heard from Judy, Mam?'

'No, Amelia was told she was on tour. Some mysterious bloke is going to try to contact her.'

'She'll want to be with Peter, Mam. There must be some way of getting to her.'

'Well Jet, she couldn't do anything if she did come. Just as well not to upset her.'

'If I was Judy I'd be furious when I did find out,' thought Jet. She couldn't imagine anything keeping her away from a man she loved. She thought it was all a little mysterious, but decided suddenly not to bother to think about any of it at the moment. Her brain and mind were weary, her thoughts had gone madly to and fro fruitlessly for so many hours.

She slept like a child. Polly had fresh clothes for her

in the morning, a real breakfast, and when Amelia saw her go into school and Jet waved cheerily, she was pleasantly surprised.

For two weeks Jet had to be content with occasional bulletins from Amelia: Peter was holding his own, still in a coma. Then Amelia arrived with a letter from Peter's mother. She found it difficult to express the gratitude they felt to Bridget. She had saved their son's life and they would forever be indebted to her. Peter was now conscious and there was a hope. It was obvious he remembered nothing of what had happened and the doctors had advised no questioning for the time being. They had been unable to contact Judith but fortunately Peter had not asked for her. They had, however, been able to make out one word he had mumbled: 'Bridget'.

'It may be that when you arrived after his accident he was still semi-conscious and the doctors say it is hopeful if he remembers you were the last person he saw. He is not yet allowed visitors but the doctors would be pleased if you would see him for a moment, in the hope that he remembers you as well as the name. We know you have done so much, we hate to bother you, but could you do this for us?'

Could she? It was all she wanted. But of course they didn't know she loved their son and that it would be a favour she was doing for herself and not for them.

James was visiting the hospital the next afternoon and Amelia took over the school for a few hours. On the way there James put Jet in the picture. It was too early to say for sure but they had hopes Peter would recover mentally as well as physically. Jet shuddered. Judy would never give Peter the care he needed if he wasn't mentally fit again. That would be another blow for him. She sent up a silent prayer. She wanted him to be fit enough for Judy to return his love for her.

153

Her heart was beating fast.

'Only for a minute or so.' A sweet young nurse this time.

She went to the bed. Peter was gazing into space. The nurse and the doctor watched Peter and his visitor. Peter's hand was lying limply on the counterpane. She thought of his hand and arm in the cold at the bend and on an impulse took it gently in hers. His head was bandaged and still but his eyes moved to gaze at her.

'Bridget.' He mumbled but it was obviously her name, and he closed his eyes. She saw the teardrops start. The nurse took Jet's hand from Peter's and led her outside. She sat on a chair outside the room and wondered what happened now. Everyone had gone off, the nurse back to her patient, the doctor down a corridor. She supposed she'd better see if James was ready to take her home. She stood up as the matron came bustling towards her.

'Tea in my office,' she said and Jet followed an efficient lady to a bright room. A kindly looking woman came over and kissed Jet.

'Thank you, Bridget, thank you.' She seemed near to tears. Then a fair-haired man, so much like Peter, came over and took both her hands. He too seemed overcome. Matron poured tea and Jet was pleased to have it. Her throat was so dry.

'Now then, to business,' said Matron. 'We wish you to come every day and stay a little longer at each visit. We will tell you what to say each day. It is obvious you are the link we have been looking for.' Jet wasn't sure she understood about the link but how could she possibly come every day? Who was going to take the school? She was about to mention this tentatively, a little afraid of the bitter disappointment it would be to Peter's parents, when James arrived.

154

'It's all fixed, Bridget. The new teacher, Miss Mortimer, will be starting earlier than we thought she could. In the meantime Amelia and Father Shields will take the afternoon periods at school.'

'Then I will go immediately and arrange transport for Bridget each day,' said Matron.

'My dear.' Peter's father turned to Jet. 'All our lives we shall be in debt to you. Anything we have is yours, anything we can do for you, we will.' Jet was touched by the feelings of Peter's parents.

'I only happened to be on the spot,' she said. 'You mustn't feel I did anything unusual.'

For two weeks she visited the hospital daily. For two weeks she held Peter's hand. For a long time he only mumbled her name, but his eyes didn't cry again. Then he said 'Thomas' and Jet had to steel herself not to weep.

On the last day she visited (Peter was well enough now to be taken to a hospital in Hampshire, near his home), he said, 'Letters Bridget, the letters.'

She just answered, 'Yes, yes, Peter,' and she bent forward and kissed him on his forehead.

There was much to do after Peter had gone to Hampshire; it was only one week before she was due to go up to Oxford. Amelia had given her the address of a little boarding house where she had stayed when Absalom was up at Oxford. Absalom and Angela were now in the East End of London, where Absalom had a ministry. They were both active in a scheme called 'The Dockland Settlement', and seemed happy and content.

She had a charming letter from Mrs Meredith. Peter was improving daily. Judith had written. She was so very busy touring all over the States, that's why she couldn't be contacted. 'She might have written me,' thought Jet; 'still I'll hear her news from Mam.'

And so to her last day at Great Little Tisbury. She felt, strangely, no pang at leaving. Not even at leaving the house. Amelia and James had advanced money to Jet for an option on the Dower House. They thought of knocking down the Plumbs' cottage; there would then be room for a tennis court. Social life was looking up in and around the village. Amelia was expecting her second child. Jet was happy to know the house would have children again. It was what it needed after this terrible war.

Her departure was strange, almost as if she'd already left and she was a ghost trailing after. Polly and Hugh were at Plumstead with Meg. She was expecting a baby at any time and Polly and Mrs Hubbard had decided to 'manage' together. Bessie, expecting a month or so later, would have helped Mrs Hubbard, but they insisted she just rested for her own event. Polly had been upset at going before Jet left ('It'll be terrible coming back after Jet's gone,' she said), but Jet hadn't minded. She wanted to be alone on her last night.

The car, which was to take her the fifteen miles to the junction station where she could board a train for London, arrived early in the morning. A damp, miserable, misty morning. Jet got into the car. She couldn't look back at the house. As they approached the bend in the lane a feeling of nausea overcame her. She felt cold and faint. She closed her eyes for a moment and as the car slowed down at the bend in a panic she thought it was going to stop. 'Don't stop, please don't stop', she whispered. The driver had seen her white face in his mirror and had been slowing down to see if she was ill. He drove on, wondering what had upset the schoolmistress. Well some people couldn't travel; perhaps she was cold. A few miles on he stopped the car and put a rug round Jet's knees.

'All right, Miss?'

'I'm fine, thank you,' said Jet.

'That's a quick recovery, thank goodness.' He knew she'd miss the train if he had to stop while she was sick.

Polly had been worried about her daughter. Jet had been warned to keep away from the edge of the platform or the train could suck her on to the line. The London stations had a terrible smell and the noise of the traffic was like thunder when you left the station. She also seemed certain her daughter would lose her way.

'But you always said, "You've got a tongue in your head; you can always ask",' Jet laughed.

'It's different up London,' warned the experienced Polly. 'There's white slave traffickers there.'

'Well, Mam, Meg and Judy have never come to any harm, and neither of them has ever mentioned such things when they've been down.'

Her mother wouldn't be calmed. 'It's different with you Jet. They like your colour hair; do anything for red.' Jet forebore to remind her mother how indignant she always got when people referred to her hair, or her daughter's as 'red'.

Her mother had been right about the London train; Jet could well understand how a poor wretched creature could be persuaded to meet its oncoming rush. And the station smell was really vile. She almost dashed back into the station at her first sound and sight of the London traffic. Her mother had advised her to take a cab to Judy's. It wasn't far and wouldn't be too expensive; and then she was sure Judy would put her on an omnibus for Meg's the next morning. Her mother had written to tell both Judy and Meg that Jet was coming for a day on her way to college. Mother had said, 'No need to reply if convenient.' Jet hadn't heard

157

and knew it was convenient. Hugh and Polly were now on their way back home. Meg's little son arrived on time, and Hugh was anxious to get back to work.

The cab driver was very kind and chatted all the way to Judy's rooms. She didn't understand all he said, but tipped him. He seemed very pleased. Judy's rooms were part of a small block in Covent Garden, converted out of an old Victorian building. Judy was 6A, on the second floor. Jet rang the bell, suddenly excited to be seeing her sister. She hoped lunch was ready, she was famished. There was no reply. Jet rang again. No one came to the door. She tried a third time, and the result was the same. Miserably disappointed, almost on the verge of tears, she turned away. There was a theatre on the corner. She wondered if they knew where Judy was; perhaps she was there.

Just as she turned away to go down the stairs the door of No 6 opened. A young woman, with tousled fair hair, smoking a cigarette, called out, 'Did you want Geoffrey?'

'No, I wanted my sister, Miss Judith Bright.'

'Judith who?'

'Bright, Judith Bright. She's an actress.'

The girl laughed, 'Aren't we all, dear.' But she wasn't unsympathetic. 'Are you sure you've got the right address?'

'Yes, quite sure,' insisted Jet.

'Well, this isn't my flat. My friend lent it to me while he is away, but I know he's had it for a couple of months. Sorry dear, can't help you.' She seemed to have suddenly lost interest.

Jet turned away. Perhaps she'd got something wrong. She wondered what to do. She'd try the theatre. She was surprised Judy wasn't known to the kimono-clad 'actress'. Obviously Judy wasn't as famous as she'd led her mother to believe. Suddenly someone called out. She turned back.

'Just a minute dear. I reckon Gordon could help you. He's lived here for ages.' Jet followed her up a flight of stairs to a yellow door. The fair girl, still smoking, banged on the door and screamed 'Gordon, Gordon,' through the letter box.

The door opened. Gordon appeared. A languid young man. Dark sleek hair, much oiled. His cigarette was in a long tortoiseshell holder. His dressing-gown was in flowered silk. His pyjamas were of red silk. Jet felt a bit embarrassed, and not a little shocked. Lunch time and both these strangers in night attire! Quite brazen about it, too.

'Where's the fire, Fee, or have you landed a part?'

Fee screamed with laughter. 'Don't be sarkie, Gord. This lady's searching for her sister.'

'Where did you lose her dear?' Gordon asked Jet. Gordon obviously thought himself a witty fellow and so apparently did his companion for they both went into hysterics at his remark.

'Don't be funny all your life, Gord. Have you ever heard of a Judith Brise?'

'Bright,' corrected Jet.

'Oh yes,' said Gordon. Jet breathed a sigh of relief; she'd just got the wrong flat. Gordon turned to Fee. 'She was in that play at the Lyric.'

'Oh, fancy,' said Fee. She gazed at Jet with interest. Jet wondered what she was thinking. Navy blue suit, flat-heeled walking shoes, round navy blue felt hat, navy blue gloves – she knew she appeared far removed from the world of actors.

'Well, duckie,' Gordon turned to Jet, 'I'll tell you what I know . . . Your sister left the flat a long, long time ago. Sometimes she or her friend (he gave Fee a meaningful look) called for the post, then she left it to Fee's friend Roger.'

'Do you know her address now?'

'No dear, sorry. I heard she got married.'

Married! Jet's mind was in a whirl. She couldn't ask, 'Who did she marry?' She already knew. It was the manner of their marriage which had shocked her suddenly.

Gordon turned to Fee. 'Adrian said his people bought them a lovely house at St John's Wood.'

'Adrian!' Fee screamed. 'I never thought he was the marrying kind.' She gave Gordon a dig. 'And you can't kid me his people had any money; Adrian was always broke.'

'Not Adrian, sweetie, the man Judith Bright married.'

Jet wanted to get away. She didn't want to find Judy now. How could she? She wouldn't be expected, probably not wanted. She thanked Gordon and Fee and left them chatting about their friends.

Her case had gone on to Oxford and she was thankful she had only an overnight bag to carry for she was tired. She saw a shop called ABC. Inside people were eating. She went in and ordered a roll and butter and cheese and a cup of tea from the tired-looking waitress. She left tuppence under the plate. Polly had advised this. She wandered along the busy road afterwards wondering what to do. She'd have to make up her mind soon. She noticed the words 'Blackwall Tunnel' amongst the places on the front of a bus. She remembered Amelia saying that was near Absalom's church. She spotted a bright-faced policeman, she'd ask him.

'Canning Town, Miss? Yes, this next bus would do. It's not a bad day, why don't you go on top and see the

160

sights?' How did he know she was a visitor? It was quite an effort to reach the top of the bus; she was terrified, it shook so. The road was going so quickly past the bus. She was glad she had made the effort for she was fascinated by all she saw. The picture guide of London Angela had sent her was wonderful, for when the bus slowed down in traffic she saw the Mansion House, St Paul's Cathedral, the Bank of England, and great buildings in a street called Leadenhall Street. Through the wide windows of the buildings the offices inside looked dark and cool; some of them seemed below ground level. Men and women were hurrying to and fro. Everybody in London seemed in a hurry. Men with top hats and papers in their hands were actually running. Some of the men were wearing suits with gold letters on the shoulders.

Suddenly the scene changed and she was in a shabby, grubby road with shops on either side. Everywhere seemed dusty and paper-strewn. And what was this noisy sausage-shaped thing clanging its way along the middle of the road, on metal lines? It swayed as the bus neared it and Jet moved her head away automatically. She could have touched it. Some dust blew in her eyes and she was searching for her handkerchief when the conductor appeared.

'What is that?' Jet pointed to the oblong machine.

'Where you bin, ducks?' For a moment the conductor was surprised, then he realised she was nervous of her surroundings. Of course, she was up from the country. 'That, lady,' said the conductor, 'is a tram, and it runs from Allgit to Cannin Tahn.' Jet told him she was going to a place called the Dockland Settlement. 'Do you know exactly where it is? I want to visit the Reverend Absalom Fox.'

The conductor was quite excited. 'Oh, old Absie's

161

place? Good chap 'e is. I'll put you off where he lives.'

He shouted over the top of the bus to the driver. Then he came back to Jet. 'Do you know there was nuthink for my kids till Father Absie came down to Cannin Tahn. They think the world of him, and Mrs Fox is a nurse you know. She has a centre where we can go and it don't cost nuthink.' Jet felt pleased the conductor had included her in his admiration; any friend of the Foxes, must be a real good person.

The conductor helped her off the bus at a place called Silvertown Way. It's name was lovelier than the place. A smell of burning soap. She found Absalom's Vicarage, and received a warm welcome from the Foxes. When they heard of her fruitless journey to Judy's they insisted she must stay the night and Absalom would take her to Woolwich, it was only just across on the Free Ferry, in the morning. She could come to the social with them this evening at the Settlement.

She said hallo to Angela's twin daughters. Lovely little girls of three, cared for by a plump cockney girl, Ivy. Absalom was not the same man she'd known previously. He was energetic, interested in all around him, untiring in his efforts for his parishioners. He and Angela seemed always to share some secret, an amusing one. Jet was glad she'd come. Amelia would be so pleased too. She couldn't wait to write to her.

She told Absalom of the jolly bus conductor.

'It's a strange anomaly Bridget. People here, who really have not had much in life, are jollier and more neighbourly to each other than people I was brought up with, people who had no worries as to possessions or material wealth. They make me feel very humble and sometimes a little envious.'

'Envious!'

'Yes, envious,' he smiled, 'in the nicest way. To an outsider, there is a roughness, a coarseness if you like, about the people here. But many have hit rock bottom, they need to be tough to survive. When I first heard of a husband and wife fighting, physically, I was sickened. Animals? Some people would say that, but between a married couple here is a loyalty and devotion and a faithfulness. Here, marriage is for life. Here a man or woman would protect their child to the death. "Our Mum, our Dad," they say. They have a sense of belonging Amelia and I never knew, nor hundreds like us. We had to settle for nannies and governesses and if we were unlucky and were in the charge of cruel ones, our parents never knew. I spent my babyhood, childhood and youth in fear; fear of my father, fear of my nurse, fear when I was fagging at school. I cannot remember my mother ever embracing me. The poor creature could not bear a child within a yard of her. Amelia was the one bright star in my life. We are both so blessed to be so happy. It behoves me to help my fellow creatures.'

The evening's social was a jolly affair. The jolly bus conductor was there with his wife and children, and introduced them to Jet. He introduced her to his mates and their families. He was proud of her and took her round with a proprietorial air. The refreshments seemed a very popular spot in the evening's festivities; strong tea, sticky buns, not a crumb left to give to the birds! Jet danced with the conductor and his mates, the undergraduates, friends of Absalom and Angela who were down for the recess and helped to make the Dockland Settlement a haven for the locals.

She was surprised to learn that Judy had been down to sing. She wished Judy was a letter writer for her letters would have been so interesting. The Foxes didn't seem surprised when Jet related the 'story' of Judy's marriage, neither did they seem too interested. Jet felt they were more interested in her and her future, hoping, she was sure, that she would make her life in that area when she came down from Oxford. At the moment she had no definite plans for her future, she didn't possess the burning desire to be a crusader in any direction. She knew she fell short of her friends' ideals and ambitions, and always inwardly squirmed about it, again asking herself, 'Why do people always want to persuade me? Why do they think my conscience should be stirred? Why do I allow my friends to give me this feeling of inadequacy?' It was like soft hands gently knocking on her mind, not painful, but irritating.

The next morning Absalom took her round East India Docks. The policeman on the gate had been at the social the night before. They saw the ships from other countries, and their crews, Chinamen, Lascars. It was all so exciting, Jet wished she could have brought the schoolchildren with her. They lunched with a Norwegian captain, Nils, and Jet received an invitation to dine with him and go to a theatre. She wished she could have accepted, wanted at that moment to be more like her sister, for there was something very attractive about the fair captain with the vivid blue eyes . . .

'He's a bachelor, Bridget,' said Absalom saucily.

He took her on a bus through the Blackwall Tunnel and then saw her on the bus for Plumstead. . . . Meg was feeding her large fat infant. His nose was tucked in the folds of a huge bosom, and he was guzzling noisily. Jet had never seen such enormous breasts. When the baby had finished feeding, Meg put him over her shoulder and gave his back a mighty thump. He belched immediately and noisily. Meg tucked him in his pram, wheeled it outside into the little garden.

'That's it till dinner time,' said Meg. The baby apparently was as good as gold; he just fed and slept. It was obvious he was going to be a placid child, and a fat one, like his parents.

Meg prepared a huge lunch; chops, mounds of boiled potatoes and cabbage. Jet protested, and was given a smaller portion but Bert came in to his 'dinner' and wolfed the lot with great applause, even to two helpings of boiled pudding and syrup. He finished with a mug of 'red' tea, kissed his wife, nodded shyly to Jet and went back to work. Apparently the firm of Hubbards was doing very well, and Jet was pleased for Meg.

Bessie came in to tea. She too was enormous, in the last stages of pregnancy, hoping for a son, like Meg. Jet was sure she'd have a son for, like identical twins, Bessie and Meg copied each other. Judy had sent the baby his bassinette. Jet had decided to give Meg some money for the baby's present. The next morning Meg's husband got up extra early to take Jet to the station for Oxford. She sat on the train thinking of her family. Meg didn't seem surprised that Judy had married. She said she'd probably married quietly in Hampshire. She had been to Winchester for a play. She would be quite happy waiting for Peter to join her at the house in St John's Wood, not lonely like most women would be. She had a wide circle of friends in her profession and in any case was often away from home. 'She would hate to be like you and me, Jet, content for our husbands to be home each day.'

Dear Meg, down to earth, placid, predictable, she searched no one's motives or conscience, just accepted things and people for what they were. She thought, however, that the invitation from the Norwegian captain very romantic and said she could see Jet sailing with her husband all over the world, a most exciting life. Jet wondered if she'd have accepted Nils invitation had she not met Peter, and knew she would, for the sailor had stirred Jet's heart in a way, but not enough, oh no, not nearly enough. She'd have nothing at all rather than settle for second best and she knew, for her, it would be nothing.

Mrs Gertrude Chambers, Mrs Gertie, as she was known, was Jet's landlady for the week before college. She introduced Jet to a fellow student, Miss Edythe Croucher-Giles.

'Call me Bob,' said that large lady. She must have been a great disappointment to her mother who, blessed with four sons, had longed for a daughter. A romantic lady who was longing for a copy of herself. 'One can dress a girl so prettily,' she had said. Her only daughter had turned out as masculine, if not more so, than her sons. She tried all she could to remedy nature's mistake, but this had the opposite effect.

Bob wore striped blouses, ties, tweed, horsey-looking skirts and heavy brogue shoes. She was boisterous and hearty. She was twenty-four. Even though Jet liked plain suits, she still felt fussily overdressed by the side of Bob. Bob took Jet under her wing, but it was hard work for Bob was a fighter for women's rights, whereas Jet was feminine to her finger tips. Bob had no need to study and work; her parents were wealthy, but the social life of her mother and her friends would have driven her crazy. The mothers' search for eligible bachelors for their daughters, the underlying vieing and competition were too much for her. She laughed about it to Jet.

'My poor Ma is lucky I've opted out. What elegant man about town would take me on?'

Politically Bob was a bit of a 'leftist', as many of the brilliant women students were and she was soon a member of various societies, including the drama society, and because she hadn't been an active member of other groups Jet eased her conscience by helping to write scripts for the drama group.

She also tried to dress as plainly as possible though she secretly thought many of the students looked eccentric and grotesque in the usual clothes they seemed to throw on, but she knew she was fortunate in meeting such women as these students were, women who would become writers, politicians, surgeons, lecturers, headmistresses, etc. Marriage was hardly mentioned among the students, it seemed already out-dated to many. They just lived with a man who appealed to them. She had so much to tell Amelia.

Chameleon like, she was sure she would become as some of her fellow students if the pressure became too great, and in a gesture of rebellion, on the spur of the moment, she went into a dress shop in the town, just to look at the apple-green suit displayed in the window. She emerged from the shop with the suit, a pure silk cream blouse, a little green felt beret pinned down with an ornament, gloves, handbag and shoes. She thought 'I'm mad. I shall never ever wear these things,' and was glad Bob hadn't seen her as she smuggled them to her room.

On the whole she was a happy student. A bit of a loner, she studied hard and enjoyed the relaxation of her script efforts for the drama girls. It was strange that, not a fighter herself, she could yet get a fighting spirit for the future into her scripts. For this she was much admired and for this she was accepted. Miss Reynolds reported to Amelia that Bridget had settled down beautifully, was, according to Miss Reynolds'

167

friend, a promising student. Amelia was pleased. She hoped this would be a turning point in Jet's life. She envied her the freedom to choose.

Jet acted the part of eagerly looking forward but sometimes life seemed unreal to her; university was more of a marking time than a preparation for any planned future. At night-time sometimes her mind was filled with thoughts and ideas from her reading. She couldn't always connect her present self with the Jet of the Dower House. She was a different woman now yet bound to that first Bridget by memories and mind pictures which made her previous self shadowy and insubstantial. This second Jet felt she couldn't suffer again the pain of the past, pain through loss; she was now protected or inured by an armour of numbness.

She saw the young Jet walking through the rooms at the Dower House, heard the laughter and voices of her brothers and sisters, and her mother calling them all in love. Then (she couldn't stop her) the other Jet slammed the front door on all those lovely sounds. For a moment there was silence and then gradually came the sounds of her childhood faint as if they were trapped and struggling to get free.

It was then that Jet knew the Dower House would always be part of her and she had relinquished it when she had no right to do so. Thomas had said it was a home for the family to come back to. But then he had always wanted Jet to go on with her education. What was she to do? There had been no other way but to sell the house.

But there *had* been another way; Hugh and the Foxes would have subsidised her, she could have repaid the loan. She just always had to be proud and independent. Judy wouldn't have done it that way. Ah Judy! She wondered when she would see them (Peter

168

and Judy) again and how she would ever cover up her hurt and envy.

Bob was a great comfort to her. She was like an older sister, as Meg had been, comforting, solid, dependable, but with the same intellectual gifts as Jet and they were both on the same plane. Bob, involved in the emancipation of women, was, in spite of her nickname and views, as feminine as Jet.

But Jet could see Bob as a successful doctor working with the deprived, as James and Amelia did now, and also as loving a mother as Jet's own mother was. All this amused Bob, and when she laughed and remarked on Jet's serious gaze on life, Jet had to smile for she was taken back to the village on quarter days with her mother laughing at the solemn Jet, the adult child.

Bob was interested in Jet's beginnings and that of Jet's mother. It was a new world to her, indeed a new world to many of the women undergraduates. For Jet and Bob began a friendship which would last a lifetime. Bob's beginnings and life were not a new world to Jet for she had learned from Amelia and her mother of so much that was similar to Bob's childhood.

The war was a topic much discussed and debated upon at Somerville. The role women had played in the munitions factories, on the land, and on the home front, had been necessary and vital to the successful outcome of the war. Their case for enfranchisement was strong, foolproof they thought.

But it was not all serious debate, although many pacifists were born at college; it was too soon after the war to forget. Undergrads had lost loved ones, as Jet had done. Visits to places of interest and the theatre came as welcome relief after hard study, and were activities of great enjoyment.

One evening Bob invited Jet to the Playhouse

Theatre. It was Bob's birthday, so Jet dressed up for the occasion, wearing her gold locket which James had given her for a bridesmaid's present. The locket held a tiny snapshot of Thomas in his army uniform. It wasn't a wonderful snapshot, but it was the only one she had of her brother. She'd cut it out of a group photograph taken in France he'd sent her. Getting ready for the theatre that evening she caught the clasp of the gold chain in the fastening of her frock and, tugging it loose, was unaware that she had damaged the tiny gold ring at the top.

It wasn't until she arrived home after the theatre and was undressing for bed that she discovered the loss of necklace and locket. She was so upset about it that she couldn't sleep. Important lectures the next day. She couldn't take time off for a locket, just a locket. Such a feminine weakness! When at last she arrived at the theatre to enquire for the missing jewellery she was sure she wouldn't be fortunate in getting it back; she might have lost it anywhere, but she remembered holding it during the last act.

'Sorry dear,' said the box office girl, 'Nothing was handed in to me.' Jet looked so miserable that the girl continued, 'Just a minute; I'll check with Mr Grainger.' She picked up the phone and had a conversation with the mysterious Mr Grainger. 'Oh, good job I checked, he's coming down.' She sounded as though the coming down of Mr Grainger was such an important and unusual happening, that Jet awaited with curiosity this visitation from above. Mr Grainger appeared suddenly from behind pink velvet curtains at the end of the foyer.

He said, 'Good evening,' to Jet, and led her to a sofa near the curtains. 'Your necklace was found, Madam, but I regret I am unable to give it you at this moment.'

Jet could hardly believe the story which unfolded. The locket had been found, not by the cleaners, but by a lady in the audience. Her skirt had caught on the hinge of the seat and when her husband knelt down to loosen the threads of the material he had discovered the locket fixed by its broken clasp to the underneath of the seat. The owner of the theatre Mr Barratt thought the photo was that of a friend who had visited the theatre recently. Mr Barratt had gone up to London that evening to a show with the same friend and had taken the locket with him.

'It was a photograph of my brother,' said Jet.

'Well by now Mr Barratt will have realised the mistake and will bring the locket back with him. I will get in touch with you, Madam. In the meantime I must apologise.'

Jet was patient for a week not daring to think she wouldn't see her precious locket again when she had a telephone message asking her to call at the theatre. The message was from Mr Peter Meredith. She sat down on her bed. Peter? Had he been to Oxford the week before she lost her necklace? Had Judy been with him? She felt aggrieved. Judy knew where Jet was now and she hadn't even called, or phoned her.

Well, she wouldn't go running to see her brother-in-law then. She telephoned the theatre and left a message. Perhaps someone would kindly deliver her necklace to the college as she would be unable to call at the theatre for some time. The locket arrived with a note from Peter. He was only at the theatre for a few days; he would love to see her. She sent a note back by the messenger, thanking him for the locket, and saying she was very busy with lectures. She hoped he and Judy were very happy. Kind regards to his parents.

She wanted more than anything to see him. It was

171

difficult to refuse. But what was the use? He was married to her sister. She had to get over it and even though they would meet one day, the longer the period in between the easier she imagined it would be for her.

The messenger returned with a short note. 'Please, Bridget, may I see you? I am off to America soon, and I would be so happy to see you before I left.' Jet felt very miserable. She couldn't understand her depression, for surely it was a good thing for her, the further away he was? It would be easier not to think of him. Perhaps she was being stupidly obstinate. Her mother would think it ill-mannered continually to snub Judy and her husband – which she was, in effect, doing. 'You're acting like a spoilt child, Jet.' But of course her mother wouldn't know why Jet was acting like this. Jet smiled to herself; she could hear her mother say, if she knew the reason; 'Well my girl, you can't have everything you want in this life, so make the best of what you do have.'

Jet surrendered. The messenger left with her note; 'I am free on Sunday, hastily, Bridget.' Jet was not available when the telephone call came for her on Saturday: 'Mr Peter Meredith will call at 1 o'clock on Sunday.' She was somewhat disappointed. Surely he wasn't expecting her to see him at the college. She decided to be ready before time, in her outdoor clothes. At least they could go somewhere away from the college. She hoped it would not be raining.

She was fortunate with the weather. All dressed, in her apple-green outfit, she waited outside the main entrance. At 1 o'clock a car arrived. The driver opened the door. Of course, she remembered, Peter wouldn't be driving again yet. He was sitting at the back of the car and made to alight, but she ran forward.

'Don't get out, Peter.' She sat next to him and he

172

spoke to the driver as he closed the door of the car.

'I thought we'd have lunch before we spoke about anything.' She nodded. She noticed the walking stick lying on the floor.

'How are you Peter?'

'I'm marvellously well Bridget, fit and busy.'

'Your mother and father?'

'Oh they couldn't be happier. They would so much like to see you again.' Jet smiled. She was just about to say. 'And how is Judy? I don't hear anything from her, but I know she detests writing letters and, too, is busy,' when the car drew up outside a restaurant.

During lunch Peter thanked Jet for the letters. He would take great care of them and hoped she would approve of the finished product, the play about which he was excited. He led her into the subject of her college and laughed at her descriptions of some of the tutors and students. He was very interested in the script-writing she was doing, but she said it was just scribbling really.

It appeared that Peter was purposely keeping the conversation light, and for this Jet was pleased. She felt stupidly shy with him and she was afraid to look directly at him for more than a moment. She smiled politely, gazed at her hands, looked round the room. She daren't look directly at him again, for when she did there was this awful feeling of weakness and lack of control over a sensible reply to his conversation. She was annoyed with herself. She knew she was acting like a gauche schoolgirl and made up her mind to leave at the first possible moment, whenever it would appear polite to do so.

Lunch was over; it was an unsatisfactory affair. Jet had settled for an omelette and just coffee, and Peter followed suit.

'It was lovely to see you again, Peter; my love to Judy. I shall be writing her. Every success in America. I'll get a bus from here back to college.'

Peter felt disheartened. For him it had been a disastrous meeting. He had been wrong all these months, not about his feeling for Jet but in his belief that she felt the same about him. When he'd seen her in her apple-green suit waiting for him outside the college, his heart had leapt, as it had done at his first sight of her at the Bull. Then he remembered emerging from that dark time of muffled pain; he'd lost his way, and it was her voice he'd heard calling him. Her hand which held his.

No, it shouldn't end this way; whether she had just been kind to a sick man, or polite to the healthy one, she should know how he felt. He felt aggressive towards her. It was her fault. He wished he hadn't met Judith and her sister. When he thought of Judith, a strange thought occurred to him. Was it possible . . .? No, of course not. Bridget was only being politely aloof because she thought he had let her sister down in some way.

They couldn't talk here in the street; it was impossible. He couldn't take her back to his hotel room; she'd never come, not this girl. He smiled to himself and wondered what she would say if he suggested it. Ah, the theatre. Claude will be there working though it closed on Sunday's. He'll lend me his sitting-room; I'll phone him.

'Will you stay for a moment, please Bridget? I have a call to make.'

Jet didn't like his tone of authority, and she wished she'd ha pencil and paper in her handbag. She'd have written one of those notes: 'Just remembered, have to dash off, hastily, . . .'

174

But Peter was back in a few minutes.

'Now then, Bridget, come with me.' She wondered where he was taking her; but round the corner, only a few steps from the restaurant, he stopped outside the theatre.

'He's going to show me where my locket was found. Oh dear, did he think I was cross about it being sent on to him in mistake?

A man was waiting behind the entrance doors. As he saw them coming he opened the doors and smiled at them.

'Bridget, this is my good friend Claude Barratt, who owns the theatre in part, manages it and also finds time to act.' Jet shook hands. 'This is Miss Bridget Bright, the lady who saved my life.'

'How do you do?' said the man. He turned to Peter: 'Did you ever find out what was wrong with the car or what caused the accident? You are such a careful driver.'

'No, it was a mystery. No reason for it whatever. It just acted like a hunter that baulks at a fence, except that I wasn't hunting and there was no fence there.'

'And it wasn't a horse,' laughed Claude Barratt. 'But the mystery deepens when, at dusk in the heart of the quiet countryside, a beautiful rescuer is at hand.' Jet settled herself uncomfortably in the chair; it wasn't the sort of conversation she was at ease with.

Telling Peter to phone down for tea when he was ready, Claude left them alone.

Peter turned to Jet, 'Why do you keep mentioning Judy and sending your love to her through me in that annoyed tone of voice?'

So he sensed her hurt. Well, why shouldn't she be aggrieved? They couldn't keep their marriage secret for ever.

'I suppose it was stupid of me, Peter, but I was hurt to hear of Judy's marriage through a stranger.'

'But that wasn't my fault, Bridget. Judith has her own reasons for secrecy.' Jet was silent. He *would* be protective towards his wife. She was acting like a spoilt child. These days people didn't confide everything in their families. Well, she had apologised. Did he want her to grovel? She felt quite tearful, she wished she hadn't come.

'I really must go, Peter, and of course I wish you and Judy every happiness.'

Peter stared at her open-mouthed. So that was it! She'd heard of Judy's marriage and naturally assumed it was Peter and Judy, of course.

'Bridget! Judy married Gerald. Quietly because of the divorce. I was happy for them. Our engagement was a mistake. It was you I wanted. That night at the Bull. You filled my mind. Yours was the voice I heard after my accident, yours was the touch which brought me back to life. Blindly I thought you knew this. It was, I suppose, conceitedly arrogant of me to assume you felt the same towards me, that the same thing had happened to you when we first met. I was going to ask you to marry me? When I saw you outside the college in your apple-green suit, my heart leapt at the sight of you.' He paused and burst out defiantly. 'I suppose I should have bid you a polite farewell today and not told you of my feelings, but now you know and I won't apologise.'

Jet never knew how she found the strength to rise from the chair, but she went towards him, her two hands outstretched.

'Oh Peter, of course I love you. I have been desperately unhappy since I met you at the Bull.' He came quickly towards her and they kissed. Jet would

176

remember always this first magic moment in her life. Her surprise that a kiss could be both exquisite joy and exquisite pain.

Peter was down to earth more quickly than Jet. He said there was so much to be done if they were to be married before he went to America; he wouldn't go without her.

He phoned down to Claude, 'I am to be married. Could we have tea now?'

Claude came up with a tray and said, 'Something stronger, surely? Who celebrates such an event with tea?'

Peter was returning to London on Tuesday. He had been to the theatre to put the finishing touches and alterations to a play which was to be performed there while he was in America. They would be away for three months, seeing publishers, visiting theatres. Jet would stay with his parents at St John's Wood, from where they could marry. They would honeymoon on the ship to America. So much to do. His parents would be overjoyed.

Jet also had much to do; letters to write, and a grim task in front of her. She had to tell the principal of college she was leaving on Tuesday morning. Opting out. Relinquishing the opportunity of a lifetime. An opportunity so many women had fought for. Who would support her? No one at the college. She was reverting to type, settling for love and marriage. It wasn't necessary, they would feel. She could write a letter explaining. No. For once in her life she should stand her ground, face up to the distasteful task in front of her. She was sorry they would think she had let her sponsors down, people with such confidence in her. Perhaps she'd even taken the place of a more worthy aspirant.

177

Bob would not understand, might even try to disuade her, bring all her big guns into an argument. No. It was what she had been waiting for. Now her life was complete; she was sure of her way for the first time she could remember.

On Tuesday morning Bob waited with Jet outside the college entrance. As the car stopped Bob suddenly grabbed her and kissed her.

'Good luck, Bridget. Don't forget me, please write. I must know how you are getting on.'

Jet hugged her, 'Of course Bob, of course.'

The driver picked up her cases. She ran to the car as Peter prepared to alight. She waved, and the car moved off.

As Bob turned to go back into college she thought of Bridget and her Peter. She couldn't recall such a look of radiance on the faces of two people. For a moment she had had a glimpse of something, something that she and her friends were missing? She shook herself.

'Nonsense, nonsense, I'm getting stupid in my old age. She went into the meeting. The subject: *Women's Rights*.

Jet was touched by the reaction of friends and relatives to the news of her marriage. They were so excited and happy for her that she wondered why she had ever contemplated a quiet wedding in London.

'Good gracious,' exclaimed Amelia, 'Peter's friends, and indeed his parents, can come down here much more easily than we can all trot up to the metropolis. In any case, how could you possibly contemplate marrying away from the school children, and what about dear Father Shields?'

Jet was thoroughly ashamed of herself. Polly was of Amelia's opinion, although she always wanted her children to choose for themselves and Hugh agreed they would help with the rushed arrangements. Peter's parents said they would like a holiday away from home, and London too.

'How much easier it all is, Mam, when money is no longer a real problem.' Wedding breakfast at the Bull.

'Yes, I'd like a half a sovereign for all the weddings Plumb and I have helped get ready. I've seen some brides do a hard morning's work cleaning and cooking before they set off for church.' Polly sighed. 'Still we enjoyed it. Sometimes there's more fun in doing things yourself.'

So Jet came down from London having bought her wedding gown there. Long, plain, stark white. Her going-away outfit and clothes for the boat and for America were ready, and Peter would bring them down when he came with his parents. He was busy with last-minute business preparations in London.

Judy and Gerald would be coming to the wedding. Great excitement for no one had seen the mysterious Gerald.

'Oh, he's a great chap, known him for a long time, you'll like him too, Jet.' This from Peter. Jet wondered about Gerald's first wife and if she was pining for him. 'Good Lord no. They are still friends, but she has her own circle.'

Jet thought this flippant. She was sure she would pine if her husband left her for another woman. She didn't say so to Peter but he clasped her in his arms and kissed her.

'We are Peter and Bridget. We are not like some theatre people. Our love will last, you know that Jet, or it will not be worthwhile.' She sighed. Of course she knew that. Perhaps she wanted all love to last and was surprised that people could fall in and out of love, at will apparently.

179

Judy and Gerald's wedding present came by carrier. Two oil paintings. Beautiful. Jet was thrilled. One was of the Dower House. In the forefront were six children. She could recognise Thomas, Meg, the twins, Judy and Jet. The other was of a haymaking scene in the familiar meadows of Jet's childhood. There were the six children again, and Jet was sure her mother and the Plumbs were there too. She loved them. For once Judy had chosen unselfishly a present that would appeal to her sister.

'I wonder when Amelia and James will move into the Dower House, Mam?' Jet and Polly were going through last-minute arrangements.

Polly looked strange and secretive as she said 'Good gracious, Jet, how should I know? It's very nice here in the lodge, isn't it?'

Jet said it was and wondered at the connection. Perhaps her mother was tired or perhaps she was afraid Jet was sorry about letting the house go. Jet was, but she wouldn't say so. She had needed the money and the fact that she didn't want it so urgently now was just one of those things.

But the next post brought a letter from Peter and her mother's terse reply was explained. Peter had refunded the option money on the house to James. Amelia and James were going up to London. James would be in charge of a clinic, a group of doctors in connection with Absalom's East End Mission and sponsored by Oxford University.

Jet's cup of happiness overflowed. She collected the keys from Amelia and went home to Thomas's house. It was shining and welcoming, flowers in the great vases. The woodwork, the staircase, the floors gleamed with shining, loving care. Jet was puzzled. Of course.

180

Where had her mother been these last few days, missing in the evening with her father? Jet thought they had been out visiting a lot lately. But they'd been getting the house ready for her. Oh, she was surrounded by love, she didn't deserve it, she couldn't take all the time; she must give something in return.

From room to room Jet went, touching a remembered piece here, living again her childhood in this warm and welcoming house. Lastly she reached the attics, empty now except for the trunks. The first four were empty. The fifth contained books. They would have to be sorted out. And the sixth. Layers of tissue paper, and underneath . . . the wedding dress. The dress, the beautiful dress the unknown bride had left for Amelia and Polly.

Jet took it out of the tissue paper and shook it gently. The parchment silk seemed to shimmer. The workmanship was exquisite. Jet took off her jumper and skirt and tried on the dress. It fitted her. She went carefully downstairs, the long skirt thrown over her arm. In the hall was an enormous mirror. Perfect! This was the dress she would wear. No one would know. What a surprise! It made her white dress look cheap and cold, yet that had been *so* expensive. Tomorrow she'd get a cab to Dymchester; she'd need a different veil, shoes and bouquet at least.

To go with her white dress she'd bought a pearl coronet for upswept hair. This dress needed something different. Of course, orange blossoms. As she put the dress carefully away, her mind was working out arrangements. She'd leave for her wedding from the Dower House. Her father would call for her there, Emily, Wally and Uncle Daniel would fetch her mother. As she put the dress away – tomorrow would be time enough to hang it up ready – she noticed another small package in the corner of the trunk. She unwrapped it; a spool of silk the parchment colour of the dress.

Mrs P had shortened the dress for Amelia and had lengthened it for Polly. She had kept the silk for any future alterations. Jet remembered how excited Mrs P had been at getting the pure silk and the right colour. She had embroidered the tiny silk handkerchief for the bride to take with her. This was pinned to the frock. Jet touched the exquisite needle work, and said a 'thank you' to Mrs Plumb for all her years of loving care.

Jet sat in the window-seat in Thomas's room. She had thought she'd never be happy again, once. Now she was happy, but it was different from anything she had ever felt before. It was a happiness which must be accepted with gratitude and not as a right. She smelled the lovely scents of the house and the countryside, she heard the voices and laughter of the children who had once lived there and, as it grew dusk, she thought she saw those children; and she knew what she must do, indeed what she wanted to do to add to her happiness.

Her Dower House would be a children's house, for the family's children, relations' children and children that Absalom knew who needed a holiday. All children should know the countryside, decided Jet, and if they couldn't have a piece of it, as she could, they'd have a sight of it, a stay in it to see the sights, sounds, the animals – their birthright.

She stood up, ready to leave. In the midst of the happiness of life there is sadness, but in her life there was a thread, a constancy, a continuation, and whatever the effort it must go on.